To We

SCOPE

Margaret Reeves

Best wishes
Margaret Reeves,

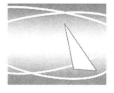

Blue Ocean Publishing

First published in 2012 by
Blue Ocean Publishing
St John's Innovation Centre
Cambridge, CB4 0WS
United Kingdom
www.blueoceanpublishing.biz

Text design and layout by Spitfire Design, Upminster

*This is a work of fiction. Names, characters, places and incidents
are the product of the author's imagination or are used fictitiously,
and any resemblance to actual persons, living or dead, or to actual
events or locations is entirely coincidental.*

A catalogue record for this book is available from
the British Library.

ISBN 978-1-907527-13-5

1
The professor's place, uphill

PROFESSOR VENABLES, an elderly slightly bald gentleman, is lying in his hammock with his eyes closed, listening to the birds singing. It's a lovely day – until Mrs Gannon, the professor's Scottish housekeeper, charges up carrying a large parcel. He can't understand why she always wears a hat – indoors and outdoors – no matter what the weather.

'Maybe,' he muses, 'she's bald and doesn't want anyone to know.'

'I'm off now, Professor.'

'Thank you, Mrs Gannon.'

'I've put your pie in the oven. You see and eat it now, while it's hot.'

'I will, Mrs G, don't worry and I've put your money on my desk. Did you see it?'

'Aye, I did, thank you.' She dithers, looking a bit undecided. 'I don't like to complain, Professor, but...'

He deliberately interrupts her. She's getting on his nerves. 'Well, don't, Mrs G. The weather's too nice to complain – too nice.'

'It's the dust on that contraption you've got on the veranda, it's ... '

'You don't have to dust the contraption, Mrs G. I've told you a dozen times.' He's getting really cross with her. 'And please remember it is not a contraption but an invention, Mrs G, – an INVENTION.' He starts to wave his arms about in exasperation.

'Aye, well, if you say so. But the dust that collects on it ... it's terrible.'

In total exhaustion he says as politely as he can, 'Good day, Mrs G.'

Mrs Gannon takes the hint. 'Aye – and a good day to you, Professor.'

Her parcel has become heavier so she makes a quick exit, muttering to herself as she walks down the hill.

Her beady eyes spotted the children long before they saw her. They were playing cards – for money, of all things. She made an effort to avoid them but was stopped by the pretty twelve-year-old girl, who said, 'Excuse me, do you work for him?'

She couldn't fault the lassie. Sally – she knew her name. Always polite and good natured despite her shabby clothes, and she looked after the little one. As for the other boy, Jamie, also twelve but big for his age, she wouldn't give him the time of day. She put her parcel down to gather herself and answered Sally.

'Aye, I do.'

Jamie was on his feet in a flash, taking an unwelcomed interest in the parcel.

'Carry it for you, for 20 pence,' he said.

'No thank you, I can manage.' She grabbed it to her and started to walk.

Jamie stepped in front of her. 'Is he batty, like they say?' He was staring uphill at the professor with a stupid grin on his face.

Mrs Gannon couldn't believe what she was hearing. 'How dare you say such a rude thing? You watch your tongue, young man, or I'll be washing your mouth out with soap.' She was really angry now.

Jamie stuck his tongue out at her. With her free arm she swung her bag at him, but he ducked to avoid it and ran behind Sally.

Mrs Gannon waved a fist at him. 'Typical that, hiding behind a lassie. She's too good for the likes of you.'

Ben, also twelve, but smaller than the others, came up to her and said, 'I think he looks like the Man in the Moon.'

She looked down at his frail little body and said kindly, 'Changing the subject are we laddie, protecting yon bully?' She glanced quickly uphill and grinned. 'Aye, you're right, he does look like the Man in the Moon.' She opened her purse and gave Ben a 50-pence piece. Looking up at Sally, she said, 'To spend on something for his cough.'

As she walked off she heard Jamie shouting at her, 'Silly old bag.' This, she ignored.

Sally said, 'You shouldn't have shouted at her like that, Jamie. It was rude.'

'So what, she is an old bag. What'll we do now?'

'Nothing, if you're going to behave like that.' She glared at him.

Ben didn't like to see them arguing. It frightened him. He said, 'How much money have we got?' He was clasping the 50-pence piece Mrs Gannon had given him. That's all he had.

Sally and Jamie emptied their pockets.

'Enough for a bag of chips,' Jamie said.

'More with my 50 pence,' Ben put in. He started coughing again.

Sally gave him a concerned look. He always coughed when he was upset. Jumping up, she said, 'I know, let's play ball.'

'That's a silly game,' Jamie sneered, 'unless you mean football. That would be okay.'

'I'm no good at football, it makes me cough,' Ben said.

Sally put an arm around him. 'When you grow bigger that cough will go, I promise.'

Ben looked at her doubtfully. 'If you say so.'

'Cor, you're a real wimp,' Jamie teased.

Sally hated him for being so cruel to Ben. In silence they followed him uphill to the village playing field, next to the professor's place.

Jamie ran ahead of them. 'Okay, I'll throw the ball and you two kick it back.' He deliberately positioned himself so the ball when kicked back would, with luck, go into the professor's garden.

Ben was anxious to prove he could kick a ball as well as Jamie, if not better. He'd show him. He ran at it with such speed and kicked it so hard that it flew over the hedge straight into the professor's garden. Out of breath, he flopped down and started to cough.

'You twit,' Jamie joked. 'Now you've done it. Go and ask for it back.'

Ben stared up at Jamie's looming body. He said, 'Not by myself.'

'Frightened, are you? Baby baby bunting ... ' He poked him and did a silly dance.

Sally dragged him away. 'Shut up, Jamie, you big bully. We'll all go.'

2
Meeting the professor

THE GARDEN GATE squeaked as Sally opened it. The gang tiptoed to the front door and rang the bell. There was no reply.

Sally whispered, 'Mrs Gannon isn't here. He's probably in the garden.' They crept round the side of the house. It seemed enormous. When they reached the lawn they froze.

'He's in his hammock,' Ben dared to say.

'Shush. I think he's asleep.' With a finger over her lips she beckoned them to follow her.

'There's our ball,' Ben said, 'under the hammock.'

Jamie smirked. 'The old guy's asleep, he's snoring.' He pushed Ben forward.

Sally grabbed him back, 'Shut up, Jamie.' The noise woke the professor.

'Yes? What is it?' He turned sideways and stared at them. 'What do you want?'

Ben couldn't stop coughing. 'Please, sir, our ball.'

'What?'

Ben repeated it with a choked voice. 'Our ball.'

Jamie pointed a finger at Ben. 'He … ' Sally gave him a hard pinch. 'Er … we kicked it by mistake into your garden.'

'In that case,' the professor said, 'if you've kicked it into my garden it becomes my property. That's the law.'

'That's not fair,' Jamie retorted, 'it's our ball.'

'We paid for it,' Ben added.

The professor scrutinised him. 'That cough doesn't sound too good to me.'

Ben flinched and Sally held him protectively. 'He's not very strong, but he'll be all right. The doctor said so.'

The professor nodded. 'Very well, you can get your ball, I suppose.'

Ben gave him a brilliant smile and dived under the hammock to retrieve it. The professor leaned over the edge and stared down at him clutching the ball. He returned Ben's brilliant smile and said, 'I'll give you a drink before you go young man – some of my honey and lemon – made it myself.'

Ben scrambled out with the help of Sally and said, 'Thank you, sir.'

'That's what you need,' the professor repeated in a faraway voice, 'good old- fashioned honey and lemon.'

The gang didn't dare move.

'What are you staring at?' the professor said crossly. 'Help me out of my hammock.'

Uncertainly, Sally took hold of his arm while Ben ran round to the other side and tipped the old man out. Luckily, Jamie managed to catch him just in time. The professor was quite shaken. He waved his thin arms in the air and said, 'Have you no common sense? There are ways and means of getting a person out of a hammock.' He grunted. 'It's a matter of quantity versus ... oh, it doesn't matter.' Grunting again, he disappeared into his house and returned with a tray of drinks.

'There, drink up.' They did. It was delicious.

Jamie finished his honey and lemon first and as the old man was busy staring through his binoculars at something, he crept over to the odd-looking contraption.

'No, Jamie,' Sally hissed. The professor turned.

Jamie said quickly, 'Mr Venables, what's this?'

The professor was quite taken aback. 'Oh dear, that silly woman and her dusting.' Angrily, he grabbed some material and threw it over the contraption. Then he made a point of placing himself between it and the gang. 'You can go now and take your ball with you. And by the way, I am not Mr Venables but Professor Venables. Remember that.'

Jamie didn't want to leave. He asked again, in his best voice to impress the old guy, 'But what is it?'

The professor looked blankly at him. 'What is what?'

Jamie persisted. 'Under the cover, Professor.'

'Under the cover, what cover?'

He's having me on, Jamie thought. 'The one you're standing in front of.'

'Oh, nothing – nothing at all,' the professor was stuttering. 'Nothing to interest you, just a little invention of mine, you wouldn't be interested. Off you go.'

The professor deliberately moved away from it to distract them, but Ben stayed put to look more closely at a bit sticking out. He said, 'Is it a gun?'

Ben jumped when the professor swung round. 'Certainly not – what would I be doing with a gun?'

Jamie became excited and gave a noisy demonstration as he shouted, 'To shoot the enemy with.'

The professor was becoming agitated. He said, 'Too much television – that's what's wrong with you young people.'

'I can see through it,' Ben called.

'What? No, no, you couldn't have – you're mistaken.' The professor pushed him towards Sally.

'But I did,' Ben insisted. 'I twiddled the knobs and saw things moving.'

The professor looked aghast. 'You did?' He quickly removed the cover and peered through.

Sally pulled Ben to one side and whispered, 'What did you see?'

He whispered back, 'People.'

Jamie smirked, 'He's having us on, aren't you bird-brain – real people was it?'

Ben could feel the tears pricking his eyes as he said, 'Yes.'

Their attention was drawn back to the professor, who had sunk into a garden chair, muttering, 'Oh dear – nothing can be kept secret these days.' He had his head in his hands and was rocking back and forth.

Ben hung on to Sally. 'What's the matter with him?'

She said, 'He's upset, isn't he?'

Ben was frightened. He said, 'With me – I didn't break it, did I?'

'Course you didn't, you twit,' Jamie hissed. 'I'll ask him what's wrong. 'Scuse me Mr ... er, Professor, is there something up?'

Ben started to cough again, because the professor didn't answer. He rocked and moaned even more.

The gang huddled together. 'Why doesn't he answer?' Sally said.

'Tummy-ache,' Ben said, 'He's got a tummy-ache.' He looked relieved that he'd thought of it.

They crept closer to the professor, whose face was contorted.

Sally said, 'Are you in pain, Professor?'

He looked up so fast that they all stepped back in fright.

'Pain?' he exclaimed. 'Yes. No, not the sort of pain you can cure with an aspirin. It's in my mind you see. I'm hurting in my mind.'

Jamie made a rude noise and said, 'Sal's dad drinks whisky when he feels like that.'

Sally was so furious with him that she stamped on his foot. The professor didn't notice and carried on talking.

'I didn't want anyone to know, you see. You wouldn't understand.'

Sally said kindly, 'Try us Professor, we might.'

'Please Professor, we're good at keeping secrets, aren't we Jamie?'

Ben gave him a pleading look.

The professor got up slowly and said, 'I don't know. It's very difficult for me to discuss something like this with you. I'm too much alone, that's my problem – no one to discuss my ideas with, you see. So I suppose things get a bit out of proportion and people think I'm mad.'

Sally put her arms around Ben and Jamie, and said, 'We don't think you're mad. Do we?'

Jamie snorted, 'Not really, I suppose.' He put his hand over his mouth and said, 'Just bonkers.'

Sally glared at him. He got the message and added, 'Just a bit unusual.'

Ben said, 'That's why we call you the Man in the Moon.' He put his hand over his mouth immediately. He shouldn't have said that and he could feel the cough coming back. The professor gave them a curious look and said, 'The Man in the Moon?'

Sally didn't know what to think. She said, 'You see, Professor, when we're at the bottom of the hill we can see you in your hammock – and you look just like the Man in the Moon.'

The gang waited. Suddenly the professor started giggling. 'Very good, very good, I like it.' He giggled again. 'Imaginative, that – and I feel much better. That's just what I needed, a good laugh.'

Out of relief the gang laughed with him. But then he became serious again. 'I think you should go home now – your parents might be worried about you.'

'No they won't,' Jamie said, 'they're not there anyway.'

The professor looked appalled. 'Not there? You look after yourselves during the day?'

Sally added confidently, 'Yes and we're very good at it.'

'I'm sure you are.' Ben's cough came back. The professor looked worried. 'You feed yourselves properly, I hope?'

'You bet,' Jamie said, 'fish 'n' chips and burgers.'

Sally added quickly, 'We're our own little family, always have been. We like it.'

'A bit different in my day,' the professor was far away in his thoughts. 'My mother was always there when I got home with a nice tea – home baked cake, jam tarts … ' He suddenly gathered himself and said sharply, 'Are you locked out then?'

'Of course not,' Sally said, 'we've got latch keys.'

Ben butted in, 'You don't have to worry about us. The Social lady checks on us.' He drew in a deep breath and said, 'Your secret, Professor, aren't you going to tell us?'

The professor yawned. 'I feel a little tired. Come back tomorrow, about the same time. Goodbye – and don't forget your ball.'

He climbed back slowly into his hammock and closed his eyes.

3
The street

THE GANG SAT at the bottom of the hill thinking about what had happened. Sally opened her supermarket bag and took out some sandwiches. As she passed them round, she said, 'What do you think?'

Jamie spoke through a mouthful of cheese and pickle. 'About what?'

'The professor – shall we go back tomorrow?'

'Depends.' He grabbed another sandwich.

Sally gave Ben a prawn sandwich, his favourite. 'On what?'

'If there's anything worth going back for.' He leaned close to Ben and tried to pinch one of his prawns, without success. He said, 'What did you see, Ben?'

'I said – a sort of gun.'

Jamie grabbed his arm and twisted it. 'Come on, tell us the truth.'

'Ouch, shut up bully.' He wriggled free and said, 'I told you what I saw – PEOPLE.' He shouted it at the top of his voice. Jamie never believed anything he said and he was getting fed up with it.

Sally got up and sat herself between them. Putting an arm around Ben, she said, 'Real people, walking about?'

'YES,' Ben gulped.

Jamie wiped his mouth on the sleeve of his T-shirt and said, 'I suppose it's worth another dekko.'

Ben looked at him in awe. 'Does that mean we're going?'

Sally asserted herself. 'Let's vote – all those in favour?'

They all raised their arms.

'That's it,' Sally said, 'we go.'

Mrs Gannon suddenly appeared from nowhere. 'Isn't it about time you children were at home in your beds?'

Ben said, 'We've been to see the professor.'

In an offhand voice, she said, 'Oh, aye, what's that mean?'

Sensing Mrs Gannon's inquisitiveness, Sally said, 'Our ball went into his garden by mistake, so we went to collect it.'

'And he's asked us back – tomorrow,' Ben added.

'Is that so,' Mrs Gannon said. 'Unusual for the professor.'

Ben chatted on, 'He's a very nice man and he's going to show us his … ' Sally put her hand over his mouth and hissed, 'Shut up, Ben, it's a secret.'

Mrs Gannon eyed them curiously. 'I know, one of his inventions. None of them work and I have to dust them.'

'This one does, I saw … ' Sally clamped his mouth again and he started to cough.

'With a cough like that,' Mrs Gannon boomed, 'you should be at home in your bed. Off you go now.'

They slowly got up. There was no point in having an argument with the old bag, Jamie mused. First thing in the morning she'd be phoning the Social, and that would make things difficult, especially for Sally's dad.

Mrs Gannon continued to shout at them. 'If I see you hanging around here again, I'll report you to the authorities.'

She hurried off, muttering to herself, 'Can't have those children spoiling my plans at this stage.'

4
The professor's place: the following day

WHEN THE GANG arrived, the professor was in his hammock. Keeping a low voice, Ben said, 'Is he asleep again?'

'Hard to say,' Sally said. 'What do you think, Jamie?'

'I know a way of finding out.' He shouted at the top of his voice, 'Hello, Professor.'

The professor's arms and legs flew in the air. He opened his eyes and collapsed back into his hammock. 'Oh, it's you. I wasn't asleep you know, I was thinking. I do most of my thinking with my eyes closed, helps me to concentrate.'

'Cor,' Jamie said. 'If I close my eyes at school, I get told off.'

'Really, even though you're thinking?'

Ben and Sally burst out laughing. Jamie looked hurt, 'I can think you know, more than you two.'

The professor clapped his hands. 'Now, now, no arguments please.'

Ben said eagerly, 'We've come to look at your invention.'

The professor scratched his bald head. 'Oh yes, help me out of this, please.'

The gang attempted to help him out of the hammock with even more difficulty. When they'd got him upright, he said, 'Thank you. I suppose it's all right but first of all I must have your promise – your solemn promise – never to breathe a word to a living soul about my work.'

Jamie drawled, 'We promise.'

'All of you, cross your hearts and hope to die – or whatever it is you say these days.' The professor crossed himself in demonstration and the gang copied.

'Good. Very well, I must take you at your word.'

He whipped the cover off the invention like a magician. 'Sit down, make yourselves comfortable.' Rubbing his hands together, he walked up and down a few times, then stopped and looked at them as if he were about to give a lesson.

He said, 'I designed and made this, er, … instrument to explore interesting parts of the world and universe.'

He hesitated and looked unsure of how he should proceed. 'And my reasons for keeping it a secret are … ' He suddenly became inspired. '… That I don't want anyone else to know, as it may be – misused.' This last bit was said very quickly.

Sally said, 'Misused – is it a gun then?'

The professor looked confused. 'No, no – it's, how can I explain - it's an electrophoto multiplier – a very special type of telescope.'

The gang looked at each other and shrugged. Ben said, 'I saw things through it. I told you, those people.'

The professor hurried on pretending not to have heard him. 'Yes, it can see at any distance and can follow the curvature of the earth – very useful for anyone wanting to observe the planets and stars.' He waved his arms around excitedly as he talked. 'By turning these dials I can get it to focus to the exact distance and direction that I want and, whatever is at that distance, you will see.'

The gang looked amazed. Jamie was really impressed. 'That's wicked, but why does it have to be kept a secret?'

Ben whispered to him, 'Because it can see into rooms.'

'Through walls, you mean?' Sally couldn't believe it. 'Is that right, Professor, can it see that much?'

The professor looked sadly at her. 'Yes, and that's what I mean when I say it could be misused by some people.'

Jamie shouted, 'By nosey parkers.'

The professor nodded. 'Yes, quite. But it is an inevitable part of the human future.'

Sally persisted, 'But it's spying.'

The professor shook his head, 'Not if it's used for the right reasons – good reasons.'

Ben slipped over to the telescope while they were talking. He turned some of the dials and suddenly shouted out in excitement. 'Professor, look … ' He began to cough and could hardly speak.

The professor jumped up and grabbed the scope from him. 'What is it?' He bent over and looked through the lens. 'Oh, no, that's terrible.'

Sally, without thinking, grabbed the scope from the professor and peered through. 'It looks like a robbery, Professor. It is – they're taking things from someone's house.'

The professor grabbed his notebook and pencil. 'Quick, give me the numbers on the dials, then I can work out where this terrible deed is being done.'

Jamie grabbed the scope from Sally and started to shout out the numbers. There were a lot of them. They crowded round the professor while he did his calculations. It seemed to take ages. They daren't speak in case he got it wrong.

At last he looked up at them. 'New York – it's happening in New York, Madison Avenue and the time there will be, let me see, about five hours behind us – about eleven in the morning, – strange time for a robbery.'

Sally could hardly speak. 'Shouldn't we phone the police?'

The professor shook his head. 'That won't do any good, phoning the police here.'

'She means,' Jamie said sarcastically, 'the New York cops.'

'Of course, clever boy,' Jamie's chest seemed to grow bigger, much to Sally's annoyance. The professor said, 'Why didn't I think of that? Where's my phone?'

They searched frantically, Ben finding it eventually under the scope's cover. The gang circled the professor as he dialled the operator. It was answered immediately. This sent him into a sort of tizzy and he started to shake.

'Get me a chair, I need to sit down.'

The nearest thing was a stool. Sally pulled it close and between them they managed to settle him. Then he went into another tizzy. He shouted, 'I need a cushion, it's too hard.'

Sally grabbed one, but they had to lift him so the cushion could be pushed underneath him. At last they succeeded in getting him comfortable, with Jamie having to be a wall for the professor to lean against. This meant Jamie had his back to everyone, which didn't suit him at all.

In his most polite voice, the professor said into the phone, 'Good afternoon. I want to make a call to the New York police. No, I don't know their number, that's why I'm phoning you.' There was a pause. He spoke again, 'It's very urgent. My number is 584321, London, yes. Please hurry.' He replaced the receiver.

They all spoke together and Jamie forgot that his back was holding the professor up. The old man fell sideways, landing on a patch of grass, gazing up at them.

The gang were clapping and shouting, 'Cor, the New York cops, wicked!'

'Wicked … they're not wicked, why do you say that?' the professor shouted.

Everything went silent when they saw him lying on the ground. He wasn't hurt, and they got the impression that he was enjoying the comfort of the soft grass. Sally had great difficulty in keeping a straight face when she spoke.

'Ben didn't mean it in that way,' she explained. 'It means, in your language, super or great.'

The professor had fallen clutching his cushion, which he'd placed under his head. He said, 'My language is the correct way to communicate. Too much television again with slang in it, please don't talk like that in front of me.'

They'd put him into a bad mood again and they helped him up, although Sally was sure he was quite capable of doing it himself. The professor left them and went over to his scope to study the dials. He said, 'That was the operator I was speaking to, not the cops … police. They'll phone back, so we'll have to wait.'

The gang were relieved that he was talking to them again. They stared down at the phone, willing it to ring.

The professor started to walk up and down with his hands clenched behind his back, deep in thought. Minutes passed and nothing happened. So when it did ring they all jumped, and the professor sprang at the phone like a wild animal.

'Hello, hello … New York police? I can hardly hear you, speak up please. That's better. You don't know me, my name is Professor Venables and I live in London, England. I have to report a robbery.' He spoke in a loud voice emphasising every vowel and consonant. 'I'm sorry, I can't shout any louder.' He was becoming agitated. 'To whom am I speaking please? Ah, Captain Murphy, how do you do. The robbery took place in Madison Avenue, Apartment 905, about five minutes ago … what? The time here … ?' He took out his fob watch. 'It's exactly four pm. My address, why? That's really not important, Captain Murphy, it's far more important for you to intercept the robbers surely? No, no, I'm not trying to do your job for you. I apologise, it's Ducks Hill, Highgate, in London.' He slammed down the receiver.

Sally cheered. 'Well done, Professor.'

'Not really, my dear. I don't think Captain Murphy took me seriously. He seemed to laugh a lot – most odd.' He ran a hand over his forehead and said, 'I've got a bit of a headache, I'll lie down for a while. I think you'd better go now.'

To Sally and Ben's surprise, Jamie went over to the professor and helped him back into the hammock.

He said, 'Can we come back tomorrow? Captain Murphy might phone back.'

The professor patted his arm with a bony hand. 'All right, but mum's the word now – you all promised.'

As they were going through the gate the professor called to Sally. 'Can I have a private word with you? Not the others, just you?'

Jamie's mouth dropped. 'I hope he hasn't changed his mind.' Ben felt the same way but didn't want to say anything, in case it was bad luck and they couldn't come back.

Sally could read their faces like a book. She said, 'I'm sure he hasn't changed his mind. You go on ahead, I'll catch you up.'

'We'll wait at the bottom, Sal,' Jamie said. 'Don't be long.'

She watched as they walked off with slouching shoulders and lowered heads, and gave a big sigh as she went back to the professor.

He had his eyes closed. He said, 'I'm not asleep my dear, come and sit by me.'

Sally lifted one of the stools and sat next to him. What was this about? she wondered. He looked rather serious. A private word, he'd said. She waited.

'I've been thinking,' the professor began, 'about you being latchkey children and looking after yourselves.' He peered at her for a moment before carrying on. 'Also someone mentioned the Social lady.'

Sally felt her whole body tighten up. He was going to ask more questions and they'd probably have to stop visiting him. She wanted to burst into tears. All she could say was, 'Yes, that's right, the Social lady visits to see if everything's all right.'

The professor pondered her comment for a while before saying, 'I don't want you to think I'm being a nosey parker, as Jamie would call it, but I'd like to know if perhaps there's something I can do to help.'

At this point, Sally gave way to her feelings and burst into tears. The professor immediately handed her a big handkerchief. He said quietly, 'You have a good cry, my dear. It helps, and when you're ready perhaps you'd like to talk about it.'

Sally was overcome by his kindness. She blew her nose and wiped her eyes. 'It's a bit of a long story, Professor – are you sure you want to know?'

'If it's going to help, yes, I do want to know.' His voice lifted jokingly. 'I don't want to put my foot in it, do I?'

Sally felt relieved that at last she could speak openly about everything. 'I don't know where to begin,' she said.

'Begin at the beginning,' the professor laughed, 'and go on till you reach the end, then stop.' He paused for a moment and said, 'That's what the King said to the White Rabbit.'

Sally didn't understand.

'Have you read Alice in Wonderland?' the professor asked.

'No, I haven't. I think I'd like to.'

'Then you shall,' he said. 'Jamie and Ben as well. I presume they haven't read it either?'

She shook her head. 'We have books at school but we never have time to look at them.'

The professor sniffed and looked away. 'The computer I expect. It's taken over.'

Sally said, 'Our teacher is very nice but the class is too big. Some days she looks worn out.'

'How sad,' the professor looked very glum. 'Is it the same for Jamie and Ben?'

Sally nodded and said, 'We're all in the same class.'

He considered this for a moment. Similar ages, so, in that case, they're not Sally's brothers. And the Social lady – where did she fit in? He was just about to suggest that Sally should go home when she blurted out, 'And my dad's not been well.'

He said, 'I'm so sorry, my dear.' What a complicated life for such a young person, he thought. Perhaps he shouldn't question her further. Then, to his surprise, she started to explain.

'It happened suddenly. One day he was all right and the next ... ' She bit her lip and wiped her eyes as the tears flowed.

Poor child, the professor mused, he'd suggest she should go home. He said, 'I think you should ... '

She cut in on him quickly. 'My dad doesn't like daylight, the doctor explained it to me. I can't remember what it's called.' She turned her head away from the professor in embarrassment.

He didn't say anything for a while. Doesn't like daylight, he mused. He'd read about it somewhere. Some people prefer the night – like vampires. Surely the child didn't think that? It wasn't true, of course, there are no such things as vampires, except in stories and films.

Sally broke into his thoughts. 'I remember now, the doctor called it a phobia and said I wasn't to worry.'

The professor patted her head. 'Quite right too – lots of people have phobias – fear of spiders, that sort of thing.'

'It doesn't stop him from working,' Sally prompted. 'He sleeps during the day and works at night.'

The professor clapped his hands, and said, 'Good for him, I work at night, nothing unusual about that. And, as you know, I like to sleep during the day in my hammock.'

Sally felt much more relaxed and she didn't mind talking about her dad now. 'My dad did try to do things in daylight but it made him feel ill.'

The professor nodded thoughtfully; the poor chap would show symptoms, no doubt, of sweating and feeling faint. And this poor dear little girl would have witnessed it.

'One day,' she said, 'it made him cry and his heart beat so fast, I had to run to the doctor's place to get help.'

'What a good thing you were there to help him. Does your mother go out to work?' The professor chided himself for asking when he saw her withdraw into herself again. He waited patiently.

There were no tears this time. She said quite calmly, 'Mum went to see her sister in Australia – she said it was a holiday. She never came back.'

'I see.' The professor now understood why the Social lady visited. He wondered where Jamie and Ben fitted into the picture. I might as well ask. 'Jamie and Ben, are they visiting you for the summer holidays?'

Sally grinned. 'No, my dad is fostering them. He said it wasn't fair for me to be an only one. That's why the Social lady comes to check, because Dad wants to adopt them.'

'How very noble of him,' the professor said.

She smiled and said, 'He's the best, and he enjoys his night job at the supermarket.'

'How very interesting, what does he do?'

'Mainly shelving, he goes around checking to see what product is getting low. He has a machine to record the numbers on.'

He probably won't earn all that much, the professor mused. Now he understood why the children had well-worn clothes, but at least they were clean; and fostering Jamie and Ben was an expensive business. But he should have an allowance from the foster care people for that.

He said, 'I think you'd better go now. Jamie and Ben have had a long wait.'

5
The street

SALLY RAN DOWN the hill. She felt as if a great weight had been lifted off her and was even pleased to see Jamie and Ben pretending to be robbers, with Captain Murphy fighting them off.

Ben's cough had started again from sheer excitement. He said, 'That was wicked, wasn't it?'

Sally patted his back. 'A bit creepy, real robbers, I won't sleep tonight.'

Jamie said, 'Captain Murphy didn't believe him, did he? It's better than telly. Look out, here comes the witch.'

Mrs Gannon walked straight up to Jamie. 'And what's better than telly?'

No one answered, which really annoyed her. 'Don't you children have homes to go to? If I was your mother, I wouldn't allow you to stand around in the street like this.'

Sally was quite calm when she answered her. 'Well, you're not our mum, are you?' But she was shaking inside when she added, 'And our home is warm and friendly and clean – and my dad is the best, even though we don't have much money.'

She put her arm round Ben's thin shoulders and walked off with Jamie following.

Mrs Gannon was rooted to the spot, staring after them. 'Never spoken to me like that before,' she muttered. 'Something must have happened.'

6
The professor's place: the following morning

THE PROFESSOR was lying in his hammock with his eyes closed. At the sound of Mrs Gannon's plodding feet, he groaned.

'Hello, Professor and how are you today?'

'I'm well, thank you, Mrs G – but I've had the oddest dream.'

The phone rang and Mrs Gannon answered it.

'Hello, yes, that's right.' She talked for a long time and the professor was getting fidgety. She said, 'What did you say your name was? Captain Murphy – right, I'll tell him.'

The professor looked at her anxiously as she put the receiver down.

Mrs Gannon gave him an odd look. 'That was a Captain Murphy from the New York police.'

'Yes, well ... ?'

She walked up to the hammock and stood very close to him. This was something she'd never done before and it alarmed him. She said, 'He's coming to London next week and would like to call on you.'

The professor fumbled with his handkerchief, wiped his watery eyes and said casually, 'Really?'

She leant even closer and said in a confidential voice, 'Are you in some sort of trouble, Professor?'

'Trouble? Of course not, Mrs G.' He gave a nervous laugh, 'Trouble at my age? You're imagining things.'

The professor looked away from her beady eyes.

7
Captain Murphy's office:
New York Police Department

CAPTAIN MURPHY WAS talking excitedly on the phone and laughing. He was reclining in a large swivel chair and smoking a cigar, with his heavily booted feet resting on his desk.

'Yeah, sure thing, it's an amazing story. This guy, Professor Venables, phoned from London – yeah, that's what I said, London, England. Anyway, I didn't believe him at first. I thought he was an old crank. But get this Herman, it turned out there was a robbery at the address he gave me – yeah – all of his information was accurate. Then, I got to thinking that maybe he's actually involved in it himself. Yeah, that's right, Herman, you've hit the nail on the head. So, this is what I'm going to do. I'm going to take a flying visit to London and check him out. Should be an interesting trip, Herman, I'll send you an email. See you when I get back. So long, old buddy.'

8
The street

BEN AND SALLY HID in some bushes and watched the man in a dark suit staring up the hill towards the professor's place. He had his back to them.

'I've seen him before,' Ben whispered. 'Well, someone like him.' He could feel his cough coming back.

The man turned and looked around furtively. He shrugged and stamped out his cigarette with his heel. Taking a mobile phone from his pocket he dialled and spoke.

'Frank, I've found the old guy's place. Yeah, sure, don't worry I know what I'm doing. I'll be in touch.' He put his mobile away and adjusted his dark glasses. He lit another cigarette and blew some smoke rings, took one last look uphill and said, 'Soon, very soon we will meet, my dear Professor.'

They held their breath as he walked past their bush. 'He's gone,' Sally said and heaved a long sigh of relief. 'I'm sure it was the man who told Mrs Gannon he was from the telephone people.'

'Yeah, you're right. I remember he had a foreign voice.' Ben trembled despite the hot day, and clung on to Sally's skirt.

'Let's follow him.' She looked down at him. 'You're trembling – he didn't see us, Ben.'

'I don't want to follow him, he frightens me. Come on Sal, let's go home.'

'It's too early to go home, besides, Jamie will be there watching telly and you won't like that.'

Ben had to agree with her. He always rowed with Jamie over what to watch. And Jamie always got his way. 'All right, but only if you promise that we won't get too close.'

Sally gave him a hug. 'Good, let's move or else we'll lose him.' They slid out of the bush. Ben took hold of Sally's hand as they ran for protection from one tree to the next along the road. 'He went this way.' She stopped abruptly and pulled Ben behind another bush.

'What is it, is he there? What are you looking at?' Ben stifled a cough and clung on to her again.

'Shush.' She held him close. 'He's talking on his mobile. He's leaning against a tree – look.'

Ben peered very carefully round the bush. The man was so close. He said, 'What shall we do?'

Sally pulled him further into the bush. It was a good big one and they were well hidden. She said, 'We'll wait until he's finished, then carry on following him.'

They didn't have long to wait. He clicked his mobile shut and lit another cigarette. He looked very pleased with himself, Sally thought. Before moving, he took a small mirror out of his pocket and combed his hair. Suddenly, he sprang round and looked up the road in their direction.

Sally held Ben close, her heart thumping. Had he seen them? Perhaps they'd better run as fast as they could in the other direction.

Ben pulled at her skirt. With a hand over his mouth he whispered, 'He's on the road, Sally, walking again.'

Just to make sure she edged round the bush to look. 'You're right, Ben, come on.'

The road was quite long. The man was making for the caravan site, Sally reckoned. There was nowhere else he could go. It was a dead end with access only to a farm. She could see the farmhouse and that made her feel better. That was where her school-friend lived. She'd been there a few times and knew this end of the village well.

She said, 'He's going into the caravan site, Ben.'

'It's getting dark, Sally, can't we go home now? I'm hungry.'

'Soon,' she whispered. 'We've come this far so we might as well see where he's going.' If she were honest with him, she'd prefer to go home. But there was something not quite right about this man, he was definitely watching the professor's place and phoning someone about it. Sally paused and held Ben back as the man made his way into the caravan field.

The two of them crept up to the entrance gate and saw him knocking on one of the doors. It was opened and he disappeared in.

Ben said, 'It's so quiet, Sally, I don't think there are many people staying here.'

Lights came on in the campsite café and some of the caravans. This made them feel better but Sally didn't want the people in the café to see them. She said, 'Bend down when we pass. Hold my hand and do what I do.' Ben nodded.

As they neared the café, Sally could see two waitresses wiping tables and cooking food. The smell of it made her tummy rumble. Safe to pass

31

now, she thought. She bent down, dragging Ben with her. They were past in a flash and found a tree to hide behind to survey the site.

Ben was bewildered. 'There are more caravans than I thought. Which one is it?'

'The caravan he went into is next to the big tree,' Sally said. 'There it is at the end.' She took Ben's hand and whispered, 'We'll slip between the caravans and go round the back of it.'

Several caravans had their lights on, which helped. Silently, they crept through to the last one and there it was in front of them, next to the tall tree.

Suddenly, a door was opened and a man's voice shouted, 'Okay, no one here.' Sally and Ben leaned back against the caravan to hide themselves, holding their breaths. The door slammed shut.

They waited for a moment, their hearts beating so fast that Sally was in two minds whether to grab Ben and run. But they didn't. They hadn't come all this way not to find out what that man was up to. She squeezed Ben's hand. 'It's all right,' she whispered.

The caravan was large, with three windows at the back. Only the one in the middle was lit and it was ajar. Sally thought if it was her van she'd have all the windows open, it was such a hot night.

She tapped Ben on the shoulder and pointed at the open window, beckoning him to follow her. All his hunger pangs had disappeared in the fear of being discovered. As they neared the window they could hear voices. One was definitely the foreign man in the dark suit and the other sounded posh.

Sally straightened up to look; she signalled to Ben to remain crouched down. There was a slit in the curtains, enough for her to see through. The men were seated opposite each other with a table between them. On the table was a case. It was open and packed full of bank-notes.

The posh man spoke. 'I'll give this to you now. You know how to use it, Mario.' From his pocket he took a box. He opened the lid and Sally had to put her hand over her mouth to muffle a gasp. Inside was a hypodermic needle. She'd seen one before when the doctor had to give her dad an injection.

Carefully she bent down and nudged Ben to follow her. They got well away from the caravan before she spoke. When they were safely back at the gate, she said, 'His name is Mario and the other man speaks posh and there's a case full of money.' She didn't tell Ben about the hypodermic needle because she knew it would frighten him.

Sally said, 'We must get home now and tell Jamie what we've seen.'

Ben was only too pleased to get away from this awful place. He never wanted to see it again and he was so hungry.

When they got back, Jamie was angry. 'Where've you been? Your dad's gone to work and he's left a list of things to be done.'

9
The professor's place

THE GANG HAD been given the job of polishing the telescope. The professor was in his hammock and they were being extra careful, to stay in his good books. After a while, Ben said, 'I'm going to take another look.'

Sally pulled him back. 'No, Ben.'

'Why not, I've finished my bit of polishing.'

Jamie took hold of his arm and pretended to twist it. ''Cos we promised the professor, bird-brain, didn't we?'

'Shut up, both of you.' She gave Jamie a punch.

Ben punched him too. 'Bully, I hate you. Anyway, I wasn't talking about the telescope.'

Jamie flopped on to the grass. 'What were you talking about then?' He raised a leg to give him a poke. But Ben was too quick for him. He said, 'The cellar.'

With a big sigh, Sally said, 'What about the cellar?'

'I've been watching Mrs Gannon.'

'And what's the old witch up to, know-all?' Jamie threw a stone at him and missed.

'Not telling you.'

Jamie started to get up, ''Cos you don't know, ha, ha.'

'Yeah, I do ... '

He pinned Ben's arms behind his back and shouted in his ear, 'Tell us then.'

Sally was at the end of her tether with them. She said, 'Look, if you keep on like this the professor won't allow us here any more.'

Jamie released him. 'Okay.'

What Ben and she had discovered at the campsite the evening before was going through her mind. They'd told Jamie what they'd seen. He'd said, 'Why didn't you take me with you?' He was obviously jealous at being left out.

'Because,' Sally had said, 'we didn't know ourselves until we saw Mario staring up the hill and saying something about the professor on his mobile.'

He had had nothing to say about that except, 'That's what we need – a mobile phone – so we can keep in contact. Most kids at school have got them, haven't you noticed?' He had grabbed Ben's comics from him and gone off to bed.

Sally had felt close to tears. He was right, most kids did have them. Perhaps, if she asked the Social lady she might help. They didn't have a telephone in the house either. She was always being asked by the school and medical centre for a number, but dad had said they couldn't afford it. He said if anything serious happened they could use their legs and run to get help. He was right, of course.

10
The street: a few days later

CAPTAIN MURPHY, carrying travelling bags, looked about, unsure of his whereabouts. He spotted a woman with a large parcel coming down the hill and called to her, 'Excuse me, Ma'am, but do you know which house Professor Venables lives in around here?'

Mrs Gannon gave him an appreciative look. He was a fine looking man. She said, 'Why, you must be the policeman from New York!'

Murphy was flattered and gave her a salute. 'Yes, Ma'am, that's correct – and you?'

'I'm Mrs Gannon, I cook and clean for him. You spoke to me on the phone, you'll remember.'

'Yeah, I remember.' He held his hand out to her. 'I'm very pleased to meet you, Mrs Gannon.'

They shook hands and then she pointed up the hill. 'That's his place, up there.'

He screwed his eyes up to see. 'Say, is that the Professor in the hammock?'

She said hurriedly, 'Aye, it is. He spends most of his time in it during the day and works at night.'

Murphy grinned. 'You don't say, a night owl, eh?'

Mrs Gannon eyed him nervously. 'If you say so, and I must get about my business now.'

Murphy sensed her tenseness. 'Of course, Ma'am, sorry to have detained you.'

'Not at all, have a nice day'. She left at great speed.

He shouted after her, 'Same to you, Ma'am.' He waited until she was out of sight, thinking 'now there's a lady with a secret'. He wondered what it was. He turned thoughtfully and commenced the climb. It was another hot day and before he reached the professor's he stopped to wipe the sweat from his face.

He was quite unaware of a man in a dark suit, wearing sunglasses, studying him at the foot of the hill.

11
The professor's place

MURPHY CALLED TO the professor from the garden gate. 'Good day, Professor.'

The professor woke with a start, looked about him, and saw Murphy. 'Good day, you must be Captain Murphy.'

'That's right, sir, may I come in?'

'Of course, how rude of me, please don't stand at the gate.' He tried to get out of the hammock. 'Would you be kind enough to help me, Captain Murphy? It's so much easier to get in than out of this thing.'

'Sure thing, Professor.' Murphy left his bags by the gate. He was a big guy and shouldn't have had any difficulty, but he did. The professor wriggled too much. Murphy scratched the back of his head. 'I reckon the best way is for me to lift you out, but you've got to remain still, Professor.'

'I'm so sorry, I get worked up whenever I have to get out of this thing. I promise to remain absolutely still.'

Murphy nodded and carefully lifted the professor, like a baby out of his cot. 'There, how did that feel?' He wiped his brow and puffed heavily. 'Not as fit as I should be, eh Professor?'

'Nonsense, you did an excellent job. You're a fine figure of a man. Thank you so much. Let's sit down, you must be tired after your long journey.'

'To tell you the truth, Professor, I slept most of the way – in between eating!' He gave a loud laugh. 'I'd appreciate a seat on your veranda out of the sun.'

'No problem, follow me. I've never been out of England. Haven't felt the need, I can imagine it all.' They made themselves comfortable on the veranda near the telescope. 'But I've been all over the world in my imagination. I read a lot, you see – beautiful books – masses of them in my library. I must show you.'

Murphy found this bit of information interesting. He said, 'That's incredible. You've never been out of the country?'

The Professor giggled. 'No – I'm kept very busy, of course, with my inventions.'

Murphy mulled this over in his mind. 'Your inventions – that brings me, Professor, to the reason for my visit. Your phone call to me about the robbery – you were right. There was a robbery at the time you said and at the address you gave me.' He paused. He didn't want to push the guy. 'Now, Professor, how would you have known that without being there?'

The professor could see the gang out of the corner of his eye. They had tiptoed through the gate up to the telescope, which was behind Murphy. 'To answer your question, Captain Murphy, let's say I have a way of seeing things other people can't.'

Murphy had to put his thinking cap on. 'Come now, Professor – you're asking me to believe that?'

Ben suddenly became excited at something he'd spotted through the scope, but stopped dead when Murphy turned and saw him.

'Professor, we've seen something,' he stammered.

The professor shushed them. 'Children, this is Captain Murphy from the New York Police.'

Murphy was flattered by the expression of awe on their faces. He said, 'Nice kids you've got, Professor.'

'They're not mine, just visiting.' The professor couldn't think of anything else to explain their presence.

Ben pulled at his sleeve. He whispered, 'We've got something to tell you, it's ... '

Jamie added quickly, 'Important.'

'Really IMPORTANT.' Sally pointed to the scope.

The professor dithered. 'Oh, very well.' He turned to Murphy, 'Will you excuse us Captain Murphy, just for a minute? Perhaps you'd like to look round my library ... '

'Sure thing, you go ahead Professor. Interesting place you've got here.'

The professor gave a nervous laugh. 'Yes – we won't be long.'

Murphy was relieved to enter the cool of the house and have a quiet think.

As soon as he was out of sight, the gang dragged the professor to the scope. 'We've seen something,' Jamie said.

The professor quickly checked to see if Murphy was out of earshot. He was. 'Yes – what is it?'

Ben said, 'I was twiddling the knobs and look!'

The professor gasped at what he saw, 'Oh, no, that's terrible.'

'What is it?' Sally asked.

Jamie's hands were shaking as he peered through the lens. He said, 'It's an aerial, a very large aerial, looks as if it's about to fall.'

Sally looked. 'There's a big wind there.'

'Where is there?' Ben asked impatiently.

The professor took out his notebook from his pocket and did some quick calculations. 'Let me see.' He gave a big sigh. 'It's New York AGAIN!'

Ben said, 'I did that with the knobs, didn't I?'

'Shush.' The professor put his finger over his mouth. 'Don't talk so loudly – top of the Empire State Building, if I'm not mistaken.'

'Is it going to fall?' Jamie's voice was scarcely audible.

The professor nodded. 'Yes, we must do something about it.'

'We'll have to tell Captain Murphy, he'll know what to do, come on.' Jamie was almost through the door but the professor stopped him.

'Wait, I don't want him to know about my invention, do I?'

Sally nodded. 'Of course not, we agreed it would be a secret.'

'You'll have to make something up, Professor,' Ben suggested.

'Yes, and you must back me up,' the professor said urgently. 'Agree with everything I say, all right?'

They nodded in silence and stayed on the veranda while the professor went into the house. The raised voices they heard from inside sent nervous tingles through them to the point where Ben began to shake.

'Captain Murphy? I've got something of extreme importance to tell you.'

'I'm all ears,' Murphy replied.

The gang could hear the professor's urgent voice clearly. He said, 'You must contact your department in New York immediately and inform them of an impending disaster.'

'Impending disaster – hey, what is this, some kind of joke with the kids?'

The gang couldn't contain themselves any longer and burst into the library.

'It's true, Captain Murphy – the Professor knows, you see,' Ben cried.

Murphy wasn't sure how to take this situation. He said, 'Knows what?'

Jamie grabbed Murphy's arm urgently. 'The aerial on top of the ... '

He couldn't remember the name of the building and looked at the professor.

'Empire State Building,' the professor blurted out.

Sally shouted, 'It's falling, there's a big wind there – and it's loose.'

The professor said quietly, 'It'll fall to the street below at any moment. The area must be cleared – immediately.'

This is ridiculous, Murphy thought. He said, 'This is really difficult to stomach. You're telling me you know that the main aerial on top of the ESB is going to drop off?'

The professor was lost for words. 'Exactly, you must do something about it. My phone, use my phone please. You've got to believe me.' They all looked at Murphy with pleading expressions.

Murphy cleared his throat. 'Okay, now let's get this straight. You've had a sort of psychic message, Professor, is that it?'

'Yes, something like that. I told you I have ways of seeing things that other people can't.'

Murphy ran a hand over his forehead. 'Well, I guess I've just got to take you at your word. But if this is some sort of joke ... '

The professor said gravely. 'This is no joke, Captain Murphy – please.' He suddenly felt very tired as he signalled to the gang to get his phone. Jamie ran out to get it from the veranda.

Murphy painfully took the phone and dialled. This game didn't make any sense, but he knew he had to go along with it – in case.

He said, 'This is Captain Woodrow Murphy, I want to make a person-to-person call to the New York Police. Yeah, Accident Prevention Department, to a Mr Herman O'Reilly, that's right. This is urgent Ma'am – top priority – thank you.' He replaced the receiver and muttered, 'It'll take a couple of minutes to get through.' He handed the phone back to the professor who was in a tizzy. The old guy needed some fresh air. They followed him out to the veranda.

While they waited, Murphy eyed the professor with suspicion. What a mess he'd be in if this proved to be a prank.

Sally noticed Ben was creeping away so she grabbed him.

'Where are you going?'

He whispered, 'I won't be long.'

'What's he up to?' Jamie kept his voice low.

Ben said, 'I've got something important to do.'

Sally hissed, 'More than this?'

Forgetting to whisper, Ben shouted back at her, 'YES.'

The professor and Murphy looked at Ben with concern.

Without being seen, Jamie got hold of Ben by the scruff of his neck. 'Such as what?'

'Such as the cellar – I'm going to take a look, while she's not here.'

Jamie let go of him. Sally said, 'It's dark down there, you won't be able to see.'

'Except rats, BIG rats, that'll eat you up.' Jamie went to grab him again.

Ben shivered and hung on to Sally. He said, 'Beast, I'm not afraid of rats.'

When the phone rang the professor jumped. It flew from his hand into the air and was caught just in time by Murphy. He answered it.

'Hello, Herman? Woodrow here, Woodrow Murphy, remember me?' He laughed. 'Yeah, I'm fine. Now listen carefully – this is urgent.' He gave the professor a last look before continuing. 'You must send a team of your men to the Empire State Building. No Herman, this isn't a joke. Get them to check the roof for a loose aerial – and clear the streets below. Make this a top priority, okay? And get back to me Herman, I'll be waiting. Yeah, that's right, I'm at the Professor's – you've got his number.' He quietly replaced the receiver.

'Thank you, Captain.' The professor spoke in a wobbly voice. 'I hope they get there in time.'

'They'll get there as fast as they can, Professor, but I must say I find this all very weird.'

With a bold voice Ben said, 'The Professor is special – he's very brainy.'

'Yes, he's good at arithmetic and that sort of stuff,' Sally added.

'That's why we like coming here,' Jamie said, 'Better than telly.'

The professor looked totally embarrassed.

They've been told to say this, Murphy mused. 'Hey, it's all right kids. I admire your loyalty and I'm not disputing the professor. It's just that you're asking me to believe – well, a bit of a tall story.' He roared with laughter. 'Tall story – get it?' They all looked at him blankly. 'The Empire State Building is a very tall building – tall building – tall story, okay?'

There was no reaction from them so Murphy cleared his throat and walked up and down, with his hands in his pockets.

Their attention was drawn to the appearance of Mrs Gannon, who scurried past them into the house, reappearing almost at once with a large parcel. She hurried past them, eyes averted, back to the street. They watched, mystified. Murphy rubbed his chin thoughtfully as he studied her. That lady is hiding something, he mused.

The phone rang and the professor rushed to answer it. 'It's for you, Captain Murphy.'

With a sweaty hand Murphy grabbed the phone. 'Hello, Herman? That was quick. Yeah? Get away with you – really? Sure, sure thing, thanks Herman. I'll be back by the end of the week.'

He replaced the receiver, rubbed his chin and looked at the professor and the children in silence for a while.

He said, 'Incredible – absolutely incredible!'

The professor spoke in a squeak. 'Incredible?'

'Absolutely incredible, you were right Professor – every word true.'

'And the aerial, did it fall?' The professor could hardly speak.

'Yeah, but they cleared the streets below in time. No one was hurt.' Murphy held out his arm to the professor.

They shook hands. 'Joyous news,' the professor said, 'wonderful.'

Sally, Jamie and Ben shouted out together, 'Three cheers for the professor – hip, hip ... ' There was a big hooray.

Murphy rubbed his hands together vigorously, 'Well, I have to be going now. It's been really interesting meeting you all.' He hesitated. 'You have a sort of sixth sense I presume, Professor?'

The professor shrugged. 'I guess!'

Murphy smiled knowingly at them as he departed.

12
The street

WHEN MURPHY REACHED the street, he stopped and looked back at the professor's house, scratched his head, picked up his bags and walked on.

Mario, the man in the dark suit and sunglasses, slipped from the shadows and followed him. He didn't know who this guy was and he had to find out, especially as he had the look of a cop about him.

Murphy got as far as the station and waved a taxi down. Mario did the same and asked the driver to follow the taxi in front.

The taxi driver, a good-natured East Ender, said, 'Cheaper to have shared, mate.'

Mario glowered at him and said nothing. The driver sniffed and whispered something under his breath.

Murphy relaxed into the comfort of his London taxi, admiring the sights as they went along. His driver, a young man, was friendly and chatty. 'That's my dad behind,' he said. 'Looks as if he's following us.'

Murphy could see the taxi behind in the wing mirror. Sitting in the back was a hard-nosed man in a black suit, wearing shades. Definitely a character he wouldn't trust.

His driver said, 'Not far to the Savoy, sir. Nice hotel, you'll be comfortable there and well fed. This your first trip to London?'

'Sure is, it's a great place – doing a bit of sightseeing tomorrow.'

The young driver waved to his dad as he turned off the Strand down to the entrance of the hotel. He said, 'Look at that, he's still following us.'

There was just about enough room for the two taxis to park and for their fares to get out.

'Thanks a lot,' Murphy called. He gave the pleasant young man a lot more than the fare.

Mario had paid the exact fare and slammed out of his taxi without a word to his driver.

As Murphy bent to pick his bags up their eyes met. He said jokingly, 'Are you following me?' He took a handkerchief from his pocket and wiped his brow.

What Mario didn't know was that Murphy had a button attached to his shirt pocket that would digitally catch him on camera. One touch of the button did the trick.

Mario took to his heels disappearing among the tourists – dropping a pocket- size London Streetfinder in his rush.

Murphy smiled to himself as he extracted a plastic bag from his briefcase and lifted the Streetfinder between the folds of his handkerchief. Perfect, he thought – fingerprints and a photo.

Tomorrow, a trip to Scotland Yard to see an old buddy was on his agenda.

13
The professor's place

MRS GANNON WALKED quickly into the professor's house, glancing around, anxious not to be seen. She crept into the back. Jamie watched her from behind the scope. She reappeared carrying a large parcel and departed. Jamie followed her.

When Mrs Gannon reached the street, he stopped her.

'Missus … ' Jamie startled her.

She said, 'What on earth – what are you doing here this late?'

Jamie said, 'I've been watching you.'

'Watching me – oh yes?' Her voice was full of suspicion.

'Oh yes,' Jamie said sarcastically.

'Don't waste my time, boy. Get home with you or I'll tell the professor.' She was beginning to shake – damn the boy.

'I don't think you will, Missus.'

'Don't you talk to me like that.'

She attempted to pass but Jamie stepped in front of her. She clutched the parcel closer. 'Get out of my way, you – young vagabond.'

He said in a peculiarly soft voice, 'What's in the parcel?'

Her anger was rising, 'None of your business.'

'But I've been making it my business – I know what's going on in the professor's cellar.' He poked the parcel.

Taken aback, she said, 'I don't know what you're talking about. Let me pass, you silly boy.'

Jamie sneered at her, 'Don't you call me a silly boy, or I'll tell, unless ... '

Mrs Gannon could feel her legs trembling, 'Unless what?'

'Unless – well, if you were to pay me something, I'd keep my mouth shut, wouldn't I?'

She was unable to believe what she heard. 'Pay you something? You young scoundrel, I'll pay you nothing.'

'Either that or I'll tell enough for the professor to give you the sack.'

She wanted to wallop him but knew she daren't. Instead she said, 'Are your friends in on this too?'

Jamie leant back on his heels and said, 'Ben knows you're up to something, but he doesn't know what – not like I do.'

Baffled, she said, 'And how much am I supposed to pay to keep my secret?'

She was giving in and Jamie couldn't believe his luck. He said, 'A fiver.'

'A fiver, that's blackmail. I could report you.'

With more confidence and smarm, he said, 'But you won't.'

Mrs Gannon was really upset. She said in a sad voice, 'I don't carry that sort of money on me.'

Triumphantly he said, 'Okay, tomorrow then – or I'll tell.'

She looked at him quizzically. 'Have you done this sort of thing before – threatening old ladies?'

Jamie looked serious. He said, 'It's not a threat, not how you mean – it's a business deal.'

'Business deal, is that what you call it?' She dared to step closer to him. 'Have you no shame?'

He looked away from her, embarrassed. 'I've never done this before and I'm not ashamed – 'cos it's not for me – it's for somebody special. I won't ask for any more.'

'Somebody special – you – what's special? ' She almost spat at him.

Jamie looked her straight in the eyes and said, 'It's for a present, for Sally's birthday. She doesn't have much, she's special.'

Mrs Gannon pondered on this new revelation and made up her mind.

'Aye, well – she's a bonny lass. Is it a promise then, you'll not bother me again, ever?'

'Yeah, I promise.'

She opened her purse and took out a five-pound note. She said, 'I must be out of my mind.'

Jamie gaped at the sight of the note. In a shaky voice he said, 'Cor, thanks, I won't tell – promise.'

He grabbed the note and ran off.

14
Captain Murphy's office: New York

CAPTAIN MURPHY WAS speaking on the phone. He was in high spirits.

'Thank you, that's real nice of you to say that. No, we're not permitted to accept monetary rewards, sir.' He paused with an amazed look on his face. 'Well, now, I think that would be a great idea – no problem with that. Can I have your name, sir? – Mario, and your other name? Just Mario, I understand. I'll contact the professor immediately. I'm pretty sure they'll be delighted to visit New York. A prize for their ingenuity ... oh, sir, where do I contact you?' He stared at the phone and shook it. 'Gone dead, well, what do you know, an anonymous benefactor.'

He replaced the instrument reluctantly and scratched his chin. He was a cop, and cops don't do business with people who don't give full information about themselves. Bells were ringing and those bells told him things weren't right.

Murphy lit a cigar and wandered over to his window. It helped to gaze out at the magnificent view of Central Park. The maples and the elms were looking good. He turned sharply and went back to his desk. He picked up his phone and tapped the appropriate button. 'Joe? – Murphy here. The caller you put through to me just now, I want you to make a check on his number and where he was phoning from. Get back to me as soon as you can.'

Maybe the guy was genuine. He hoped he was. It would be great for the kids to visit New York, and company for Dwight. They'd stay in his apartment, of course, and he'd take some leave to accompany them on days out. He'd arrange for a team of plainclothes cops to be with them all of the time.

He returned to the window and looked down at the Park. Plenty for them to do in there and the crime figures had dropped – that was good.

The phone rang. It was Joe with bad news. 'You couldn't trace it – nothing at all?' He listened while Joe talked of other options. 'There's the recording, Captain Murphy, shall I send it up to you?'

'Do that Joe, and thanks.'

While he waited for it to arrive, Murphy phoned his home. He'd have to work late tonight to get this benefactor sorted out in his mind. There was no reply from Dwight; then he recalled that his son was staying over at Brad's tonight. He needn't have worried.

There was a tap at the door. Murphy returned to his desk and called, 'Come in, Joe.'

Always in a hurry and eager to please, Joe deposited the recording on the desk. He said, 'There's something else for you.' He dug into his hypermarket basket and produced a package. 'It was sitting on my desk. Don't know how it got there. The post room finished an hour ago.'

Murphy picked it up carefully. He said, 'So it hasn't been through the usual security check?'

'Couldn't have,' Joe speculated, 'it's not stamped.'

'How do you know it's for me?' Murphy asked. 'There's no writing on it.'

'Ah,' Joe laid the basket down rather heavily on Murphy's desk and took a sheet of paper from his pocket. 'That was on top of it.'

Opening a drawer in his desk, Murphy took out his protective gloves and put them on before taking it from Joe. He scrutinised the sheet thoughtfully. 'Usual anonymous style,' he murmured. His face became serious.

Joe said, 'Something bothering you, Captain Murphy?'

Murphy leaned forward and picked up a large magnifying glass. 'Nothing for you to worry about, Joe. Time for you to go home, isn't it?'

Joe nodded. He was reluctant to leave, especially when the Captain had something juicy sitting on his desk.

With tongue in cheek and not bothering to look up, Murphy said, 'It's about time you returned that hypermarket basket, to its legal owners, Joe.'

'Oh, come on boss,' he wailed, 'I'm fond of this old basket and it's better than any mail bag the NYPD have come up with.'

Murphy made no comment and waved him off.

As soon as Joe had closed the door behind him, Murphy opened the package. He was sweating and his heart was beating heavily. By the time he'd got the layer of brown paper removed, he sat back and breathed in deeply several times. Thank God, he thought, it would have exploded by now if there had been a bomb. Lying in front of him was a plastic bag which contained three return air tickets, London–New York–London, for minors. Below the tickets was a cheque for a considerable amount of cash. So, money was no object to the anonymous benefactor.

He placed the tickets and cheque in his desk and picked up the disk of Mario's conversation. He put it in his machine. Before turning it on he put two large ice cubes into a glass and poured himself a double whisky. He needed it.

He listened intently; the whisky was working and he relaxed. The second time around, he noticed that Mario dropped his h's. He made a note of it. And the third time around, something which hadn't connected before, were the background noises. With careful manipulation of the machine, which could raise or lower the tempo at any particular point, he was able to comprehend a variety of background sounds. He fished around in his desk for the special earplugs that would enhance the sounds, poured another whisky and locked the office door. He didn't want to be interrupted. He sat at his desk, closed his eyes and pressed the button to listen. Now he was totally focused. He smiled each time his eyes flew open to make notes. The call had come from an enclosure of some sort – he could tell from the acoustics – near Big Ben, whose chimes were muffled. Mario was not alone. A posh voice said one word: 'finish'. Finish what? The phone call maybe? Yeah, of course, he was on his cell phone. Another voice said, 'Fourth floor.' The enclosure was an elevator. They got out at the fourth floor. The posh voice said, 'Room 415.' They were in a hotel. Now, Murphy wondered, how many hotels are there, near Big Ben in London, with a Room 415? Masses!

15
The professor's place

THE PROFESSOR WAS talking excitedly to the gang. Unseen by them, Mario was hidden in a shadowed area behind some bushes, listening.

'And that's it. I had a telephone call from Captain Murphy. It appears that a gentleman in New York was so grateful for our warning that he wants to give us a reward – and that reward is a trip to New York.'

Ben shrieked with delight, 'Can't believe it, New York.'

Sally and Jamie joined in. 'It's like a dream – really great.'

The professor clapped his bony hands to see the gang so happy. He said, 'When you get back you must tell me all of your exciting news.'

Disappointed, Ben said, 'Aren't you coming, Professor?'

'No, I won't be, Ben. I've never travelled abroad and I don't intend starting now.'

Sally and Jamie couldn't believe it. They said it was his invention and that he should. And what should they do if they were asked questions, because people would know if they were lying.

'You don't have to lie,' the professor said. 'Just say that I have the power to see things other people can't.'

In anguish, Jamie added, 'And you reckon they'd believe us?'

'It's the truth,' the professor looked confused. He hadn't taken this into account. They were right, of course. He passed it off with a wave of his hand, 'I have the power through my invention – you don't say anything about it, it's simple.'

He felt even more confused now and so did the gang. Best change the subject, he thought. He patted Ben's head and said, 'You know, young man, you haven't coughed so much recently, you must be getting better.'

Ben agreed. He said, 'I'd feel even better if you were coming with us.'

The professor really didn't want this problem. He'd have to be tough with them. 'Nonsense, you don't need me, off you go now. It's all arranged. Go and get your packing done.'

With great effort, he shovelled them out of his garden and waited as they ran down the hill. At the bottom they turned and waved, and he waved back vigorously. With a contented sigh he returned to his hammock.

Mario waited until the professor had made himself comfortable before slipping out from behind the bushes. He trod slowly up to the hammock. The professor had his eyes closed. Had he fallen asleep that quickly? Mario spoke in a not unpleasant loud voice.

'Professor Venables?'

The professor's eyes flew open and he looked straight into a pair of dark glasses.

'Good heavens, who are you?'

Mario gave him his most charming smile. 'Let's say, an old friend – no, better than that – your benefactor.'

The professor turned his head away from the dark glasses and said, 'If you're a salesman, I don't need anything, thank you. Now, you found your way in, so I presume you can find your way out. Good day.'

Mario raised his arms in the air. 'You don't understand, Professor. I'm the gentleman from New York.'

The professor turned his head to look at him again.

Mario continued to speak in a most pleasant tone. 'I put up the reward money – Captain Murphy phoned you.'

The professor gasped. 'I see. Please would you help me out of this hammock?'

This didn't suit Mario at all. He groaned to himself. It was lowering for him to lift an old man like a baby out of his cot. But time was getting short so he'd have to get on with it. He removed his immaculate jacket and sunglasses and with a sweep of his arms lifted the old man on to the grass.

The professor was amazed. He said, 'You must think me rude. Can I get you a drink?'

Mario declined. 'I'll come straight to the point, Professor. I want to discuss a little business transaction with you.'

He followed the professor on to the veranda, where they sat close to the scope. His sharp eyes scanned the object for clues while he continued to talk.

'My government are prepared to pay you a considerable amount of money for your invention.'

The professor looked blankly at him, 'Invention – what invention?'

Mario gave a false laugh. 'Come now, Professor, let me jog your memory – New York, the Empire State Building?'

The professor retained his blank face. 'I don't know what you're talking about. I find this very upsetting.'

Mario wiped the sweat from his forehead with a large silk handkerchief. He said casually, 'Rumour has it that you have designed – created a vitally important piece of defence equipment. Put in the wrong hands it would be lethal, but in the right hands it would have far-reaching worldwide benefits.'

Totally confused, the professor said, 'How did you come by this information?'

Mario was in his element as he explained cynically to the old man that walls have ears; about his long conversations with physicists and mathematicians. The professor listened with his mouth hanging open as he continued to talk. 'We have all the tapes. But what we don't have are statistics, plans, codes and, of course, the scope itself.'

When Mario paused to light a cigarette, the professor said, 'My phone bugged – how?'

Mario blew smoke rings at him and said, 'You sleep too well in your hammock, Professor. A telephone engineer comes and goes very quietly – beyond suspicion.'

The professor managed to gather himself. 'I don't know what you're talking about. So far as my invention is concerned, I've burned all my papers. Too much mess about the place. As for my telescope – I study the stars.'

He could see Mario was losing patience.

'Don't waste my time, Professor. Name your price. My government will be generous.'

The professor was losing his patience too and told Mario he intended to inform the police of his harassment. Mario sneered and said that his government would stop at nothing to obtain the information, did he make himself clear?

'Not particularly,' the professor shrugged.

Mario had great difficulty in controlling himself. 'I'm sorry, Professor. Perhaps I haven't explained things clearly – accept my apologies. I'll contact you again in two days.' He got up to go. At the gate he turned and called, 'One other thing, our conversation today is of the utmost importance to my government. You will appreciate that our talk must remain completely confidential. If you were to contact the police for instance, considerable misunderstandings might result. Good day, Professor.' In his hurry to depart, Mario nearly collided with the gang.

Jamie shouted, 'Watch it, mate.'

'I've seen him before somewhere, odd looking guy,' Sally said. He was the same man in the caravan, but she daren't let on. Now wasn't the time. Luckily, Ben hadn't seen him that close.

'I remember,' Ben said, 'he was the telephone man.'

Jamie was desperate to change the subject. 'Sally, me and Ben have got a pressie for you.'

She blushed, 'It isn't my birthday until tomorrow.'

Ben tugged at Jamie's sleeve and whispered, 'What is it? I don't know anything about it.'

Jamie hissed at him, 'Pretend you do, bird-brain.'

Ben shrugged as Jamie handed her the parcel. When Sally opened it she screamed with delight. 'It's the blouse from the market. You didn't pinch it, did you?'

Jamie looked hurt. 'Of course we didn't.' He shuddered when he remembered how he got the money.

Sally apologised and asked if they'd knocked the price down. She knew it was expensive. They must have used up all their pocket money.

'There's a bit left over. We've been saving for a long time,' Jamie said. 'We knew you wanted that blouse.'

He gave Ben a poke.

'Yes,' Ben spoke with rather too much gusto. 'We knew you wanted it badly.'

Sally said, 'I can wear it to New York.' Blushing again, she gave them both a quick kiss.

'That's right – New York here we come,' Jamie shouted.

Unobserved, the professor had been listening to their conversation. He was glad they'd been given the opportunity to see another part of the world, but he feared for their safety. The Mario person was a devious character. Perhaps he should contact Captain Murphy and warn him. The children were calling him, he must go to them. It was difficult to be cheerful when the circumstances were grim. He put on his best smile and said, 'Ready to go, packing done?'

Sally gave him a sad look. 'Yes, we're ready. Are you sure you won't come with us?'

The professor coughed and rubbed his hands together, 'Absolutely. Now, don't forget to send me a card. Promise?'

'We promise.' Ben wanted to cry when Sally gave the professor a big hug and kiss and Jamie shook his hand.

There was a sound of tooting. 'That'll be your Social lady,' the professor said, as he shuffled them through the gate and waved them off. He waited until they were out of sight before hurrying to his phone. He picked it up, thought for a moment, changed his mind and put it down. He rushed into the house and returned very quickly with large cardboard boxes, and began packing bundles of papers into them.

I'm in a bit of a tizzy again, he thought. There had been so much preparation for the gang's flight to New York. At least he'd had the opportunity of meeting the Social lady, a Miss Turner. That had been a surprise. There had been an awful lot of forms to fill in. She'd been very helpful and long suffering. He wondered about Sally's dad. He had the job of arranging for passports and special documents for unaccompanied children with the air company. He thought Miss Turner would arrange a meeting for him with the dad, but she didn't. Oh well, at least they were on their way. It was Miss Turner's responsibility to see them safely to the airport, where she would hand them over in a special lounge set apart for that sort of thing to a hostess whose job it was to care for them on the aircraft.

When they reached New York airport they'd be met by Captain Murphy and they'd be in safe hands.

Two days later

Mrs Gannon arrived unusually early, much to the professor's relief. He had the boxes ready for her to burn. The one and only remaining copy of his calculations and drawings he'd placed in a safe deposit box in his bank.

She was unusually cheery. 'Good morning, Professor.'

He found her bright spirits annoying. 'Good morning, Mrs. G.' He spoke very quietly and continued to throw more papers into more boxes.

Mrs Gannon was surprised to see him tidying his papers up. 'Anything wrong, Professor?'

He didn't look at her but carried on packing, 'Just tidying a few things away.'

Mrs Gannon stared around the veranda. 'Where's your contraption?'

At last he turned and looked at her. 'Do you mean my invention? I've taken it apart – it's in that box.' He pointed to a long box, which usually held heavy gardening equipment. He plunged the cardboard boxes into her arms. 'Take them, Mrs G, please. Useless papers I want to get rid of. Put them in the incinerator.'

Mrs Gannon was mystified and didn't move. The professor said, 'Now, please, I'm expecting a visitor in a few minutes. I think a cup of tea might be needed.'

She was about to say something but changed her mind. Strange, she thought, that the professor is burning his papers.

Left alone, the professor checked around to make sure not one piece of evidence was left lying. He climbed wearily into his hammock, mumbling to himself, 'I think that's everything'. He closed his eyes but found it hard to relax.

The squeak from his garden gate warned him that his visitor had indeed arrived. He daren't open his eyes but he could hear the soft tread of feet getting closer.

'Good morning, Professor.'

He answered in a faint voice. 'Is it a good morning?'

Mario ignored this comment. He placed his case down in such a way for the professor to be able to see, without difficulty, what it contained.

'Well, Professor, I've given you the two days and, before you say anything, let me show you this.'

Mario opened the case filled with bank-notes. He spoke in a quiet clipped voice. 'One million pounds, Professor and more if you co-operate.'

The professor said casually, 'Can I smell burning?'

Mario felt his anger returning. 'Don't waste my time, Professor, your decision please.'

The professor deliberately played for time, pretending to think. Unnoticed by Mario, Mrs Gannon returned and saw the case full of money. She held her hand over her mouth for fear of disturbing the stranger. The professor had seen Mrs Gannon out of the corner of his eye, and answered Mario's question like a naughty schoolboy.

'NO.'

Mario looked at him fixedly. 'Is that your final word?'

'YES.'

'That's too bad.' Mario bent down and opened a flap in the case, taking out a hypodermic syringe. He held it in front of the professor's face so he could get a good look at it. 'Just one injection of this, Professor, and you will pass away from what the Coroner will call 'natural causes'. I will search and find what I want and you will be dead to the world.' While Mario was talking, Mrs Gannon slid the scope from its box. 'What a pity. I will give you one last chance – one minute precisely, to reconsider.'

Mario checked his watch. The professor could see Mrs Gannon lifting one end of the scope. She had it raised above her head and was creeping up behind Mario.

The professor shouted out, 'I repeat, NO.'

Mario grabbed hold of his arm and raised the syringe. 'Don't bother to struggle, Professor, I'm so much stronger than you.'

Mrs Gannon crashed the scope down on Mario's head. Shaking, she stared at the crumpled body lying at her feet. 'Is he dead?'

The professor cried out in relief, 'Of course he isn't dead. Well done, Mrs. G. Quick, help me out of this hammock, we must phone the police before he comes round. Come on.'

Mrs Gannon couldn't stop shaking. 'What a terrible thing this is ... yes, the police.

As soon as he was upright the professor said urgently, 'Where's the phone?' He couldn't see it anywhere.

Mrs Gannon was still in a state of shock, and wandered round aimlessly looking for it.

The professor was getting angry with her. 'Mrs G, gather yourself, please. Where is my phone?'

She said, 'I don't feel well, Professor. I must go to the bathroom.' With a hand over her mouth she ran into the house.

The professor pursued her, shouting, 'My phone, Mrs G!' He stood outside the bathroom, banging on the door. He could hear her retching. What a time to be sick. Then he heard a weak voice telling him where she'd plugged it in. He flew to the kitchen as fast as his poor legs would allow, muttering to himself that Mrs G was becoming a liability, phoning friends all the time. His telephone bill was getting bigger with each month. He'd put a padlock on it.

With a shaking hand he called 999. This was definitely an emergency. It was answered immediately. What luck. He said, 'I wish to report an attempt on my life. The person involved is lying in my garden in a state of unconsciousness – we knocked him out.' They seemed to be asking an awful lot of questions. He said, 'This is an emergency. Please send a policeman to my house now.' He slammed the phone down in such fury that the instrument broke into pieces.

Mrs Gannon's voice behind him increased his tizzy. She said, 'Professor, what have you done?' She took an old newspaper from a pile and spread it on the kitchen table, then made a neat parcel of the pieces. 'Perhaps it can be mended.'

The professor drew in a deep breath and said, 'The police are on their way, Mrs G, and we should go back to the garden and wait for them there.' He turned sharply and signalled Mrs Gannon to walk ahead of him. If she was going to be sick again on encountering the body, best to get it over and done with before they arrive.

A shocked scream from Mrs G was not what the professor expected. She said, 'It's gone – he's not there.'

'Gone? He can't have gone, he was unconscious!' The professor rushed round the garden. 'Perhaps he's partly conscious and crawling into a bush.'

Further searches proved that the fellow Mario had disappeared, complete with his case of money and horrible needle.

Out of breath, the professor flopped into his hammock. 'A drink, Mrs G, please – I need a drink.'

'Not before I've tidied your contraption away.'

He screamed at her, 'Don't touch anything. It's vital evidence.' His legs flew into the air and tipped him out of the hammock. He was at her side in no time. 'Have you touched the scope?'

'You told me not to, so I haven't.' Mrs Gannon marched into the house and returned almost immediately with large glasses of orange juice. They drank in silence. The drink was definitely needed.

Partly refreshed, the professor got down on his hands and knees and began crawling around, studying every blade of grass through a large magnifying glass.

Mrs Gannon said, 'What are you looking for?'

He didn't answer her but carried on with his inspection of the lawn. At the sound of a car approaching he jumped to his feet. 'That'll be the police,' he said.

'You look very odd,' Mrs Gannon said critically. 'You've got green knees and green elbows. Why are you wearing your white suit anyway? Wimbledon's been and gone.'

'Because I like my white suit – is that good enough for you?' Thankfully, he heard the gate latch being lifted quietly and prepared himself to welcome his guests with a pleasant smile.

Much to his disappointment, a young man in police uniform approached him. He looked like a boy. Surely this fellow isn't properly trained to catch an international spy!

The young constable smiled warmly. 'Good morning, Professor. You reported a spot of bother I understand.' He took out his black notebook and pencil and waited. Looking at the professor's unusual suit, he said, 'Nice day for gardening, sir.'

'Yes, I mean no, Constable. I haven't been gardening. Would you like to sit down and partake of a cup of tea with us, on the veranda of course?'

'That would be very nice, Professor.' He sat himself in the shade and removed his hat.

The professor grunted to himself. He's removed his hat, part of his uniform. Surely when making enquiries about possible espionage he should be in full uniform?

Mrs Gannon appeared with a tray of tea and biscuits and poured. Considering the serious nature of what had taken place, she mused, nothing much was happening.

When he'd finished his tea, the constable said, 'Now, Professor, if you could tell me exactly what took place please.' He held his black notebook at the ready.

'Of course.' The professor rose briskly from his chair and positioned himself on the lawn next to his hammock.

The constable noticed how the professor took a wide circle around an odd piece of tubular metal lying on the lawn. He made a note of it.

This didn't go unnoticed by the professor. He was pleased. Perhaps this young chap was going to be reliable after all. He then went into lengthy detail regarding the history of the man in the dark suit, of how his government was keen to obtain his invention complete with all drawings and calculations.

The young constable's arm was beginning to ache. He wished the professor would be less colourful about – everything! When it came to the case full of money and the hypodermic syringe, he found it hard to keep a straight face. One hour later he closed his notebook with relief.

The professor returned to his chair on the veranda, satisfied that he had presented the perfect seminar, reminding him of the old days. Mrs Gannon had fallen asleep. He gave a big cough, which wakened her.

She blinked and said, 'Have you finished, Professor?'

'I have, Mrs G.' He waited for the constable to summarise his findings.

Much to the professor's distress, he pocketed his notebook, stood up and replaced his hat.

The constable said, 'I've made a note of everything you've said, sir, and I'll get back to you – about the middle of next week.'

'Is that all? What about taking samples and swabs?' The professor was shocked.

The constable looked thoughtfully at the area of the alleged attack. He then walked around it, staring down at the grass and briefly at the odd piece of tubular metal. He said, 'I see no evidence of the grass being disturbed by a body lying on it, having been coshed.'

'But what about the tube?' the professor demanded, 'It's part of my invention, shouldn't it be taken to your lab for tests?' He turned to Mrs Gannon. 'Tell the constable, Mrs G, exactly what you did with the scope.'

She nodded. 'I picked it up and hit the man over the head and knocked him out.'

The constable tutted. 'If that is the case, Mrs Gannon, and the man is around to confirm that that is what you did, I'd probably have to take you with me, charged with GBH.'

'GBH, what on earth is that?' the professor asked urgently.

'Grievous Bodily Harm, sir.' He hesitated and added, 'If you'd just give me a moment, sir, I have equipment in my car which I can use to look very closely at the tube.'

The professor held his hands together as if he were praying. 'Thank goodness, and what will you be looking for?'

He said, 'Fingerprints, hair, blood and if necessary, a swab for DNA purposes.'

At the gate he turned and said, 'Has anyone else touched the tube?'

'Mrs Gannon, of course, her fingerprints will definitely be on it.'

He nodded and left them. The professor and Mrs Gannon studied the tube. She said, 'It was always my practice to keep it smart, so it should show up all those things he was talking about very clearly.'

The constable returned with quite a large box. Taking a pair of white gloves out of a plastic bag he put them on, then proceeded to do various close tests with an instrument the professor was not familiar with. He was very thorough, something that he appreciated.

The constable's final inspection was to lift the tube upright. He handed a pair of white gloves to the professor and asked him to hold the tube still while he repeated the tests on the side that had lain against the grass.

At the end, he removed his gloves and made more notes in his black book. He looked up and said, 'It's absolutely clean, no fingerprints, nothing.'

The professor sat down slowly and put his head in his hands.

The constable felt sorry for him. 'Just to put your mind at rest, sir, I'll take the piece of tube with me and have the tests repeated.'

The professor mumbled a thank-you.

Turning back to Mrs Gannon, the constable said, 'What does he do for a living?'

Mrs Gannon shrugged and said, 'He invents things.'

16
New York

CAPTAIN MURPHY MADE SURE he was at the airport in good time. He was thinking about his trip to London and the taxi that had followed him to the Savoy. He'd met up with his buddy at Scotland Yard, who'd arranged for the fingerprints and photos of the dubious looking guy he'd encountered outside the hotel to be checked.

He was not surprised at the information that had come through that very morning. The fellow had a long cop record throughout Europe and further afield, including the USA. He travelled around under many aliases and disguises as an international spy. Born in the Ukraine, he wasn't married, spoke six languages fluently and was known to be involved in terrorist activities. So far, he'd been difficult to pin down, mainly due to unscrupulous lawyers finding the perfect exit, at a cost.

What excited Murphy was the guy's latest alias name – Mario. He was pretty sure that the Mario who had phoned him and the Mario in London were one and the same.

Murphy had just one thing on his mind – the safety of the children. To this end, during their stay in New York, they would travel around only in a NYPD car, driven by himself or his second in command. His apartment in Manhattan was considered to be a safe house, with a bullet-proof main door and windows. During the kids' stay there would be at least two cops on duty day and night.

Over the Tannoy he heard the announcement of the arrival of the flight from London. The children wouldn't be accompanied through the usual arrivals channel; he was to go to a special lounge and pick them up. Murphy casually glanced around as he walked. He was surrounded by four of his men in plain clothes. For himself, he was in full NYPD uniform. That's how he wanted it and he knew the kids would like it too.

Lillian, the hostess on the aircraft who was looking after them, said, 'We wait until all the passengers have left the aircraft.' Sally loved to listen to her American voice, it was gentle and she had beautiful teeth, so white.

It took ages for the passengers to get off. Ben had slept a lot during the flight, but Jamie's eyes remained wide open taking in every detail, especially when the grub arrived. He thought Lillian was very pretty, a bit like the girls on telly, but not as pretty as Sally, she was the best.

Lillian left them briefly to have a word with the pilots. They were very close to the cockpit and when she opened the door, Jamie had never seen so many dials and buttons and other things, except at the professor's. She had to unlock and lock the door when she went in and out. He wondered why that was.

When Lillian returned she had a bag of goodies for each of them. She said, 'We can go now to meet your friend, Captain Murphy.'

Sally couldn't believe they were in New York. They followed Lillian down the steps on to the tarmac.

Everything seemed so large; the aircraft was huge. Even the people looked large! At the foot of the steps, a car was waiting. That was large as well. Jamie said, 'It's called a limo.'

'It's very noisy here,' Ben said. They clambered into the back of the limo and were surprised to see their baggage was already on their seats.

Ben said to Lillian, 'Why are we going by car? The other passengers are walking to the building.'

Lillian gave him a little hug. He was a sweet little boy but he had coughed a lot on the aircraft, so she'd given him a mild sedative and that had worked. 'You're going by car because you are being met by a very important man.'

'Captain Murphy,' Jamie shouted. He nudged Ben who still looked a bit bleary-eyed from whatever she'd given him.

Their car journey was short, round the building to a back door. Walking through it they found themselves in a corridor that led to a very smart lounge. Jamie noticed a man in plain clothes standing outside the door, looking up and down the corridor. Inside was Captain Murphy in full cop uniform. They were so pleased to see him.

Lillian watched engrossed as they ran to him. She knew the background of the children, Miss Turner at London Airport had been most informative. No doubt they'd meet up again when she returned them in two weeks' time. She slipped quietly from the lounge; her part of the job had been completed successfully.

'Hi, kids.' Murphy opened his arms wide so he could embrace them at one go. He was a big guy and had no difficulty in achieving that feat. Sally and Ben were closest to his chest, while Jamie held back just a little bit. But that was to be expected. Although all three were the same age, Jamie saw himself as the senior of the trio.

Murphy said, 'We'll go straight to my car and I'll take you home. Then you can tell me all about your first experience of an aircraft and New York!'

'Our bags,' Sally said.

'No problem, at this moment they're already sitting on the back seat of my vehicle.'

As they were talking, Jamie noticed the pilots from their aircraft walking into the lounge. They looked really smart. Perhaps I could be a pilot one day, he thought. He went over to the one with the most bands round his jacket cuff. He must be the important one. He said in his best English, 'Please, sir, would you sign my autograph book for me?'

The pilot looked chuffed at his request. 'Sure will,' he said, 'never been asked for an autograph before.' He turned the pages and said, 'I guess I'm your first?'

'Not quite,' Jamie said, 'Lillian signed for me. In the centre pages – 'Now please do not fiddle, 'cos I'm in the middle.' He flushed and the pilot patted his shoulder.

Murphy called to Jamie as he gave a thumbs-up to the pilot. The gang followed him through another door that connected to the main concourse. It was crowded with people coming and going. Jamie noticed, once again, that Captain Murphy was surrounded by men in ordinary clothes constantly looking about them. He was important, he supposed, and had to be protected, just like on the telly.

Beyond large sliding doors sat a limo with the initials NYPD written on both sides. One of the plainclothes men opened the door for them and they climbed in. There was another guy on the other side of the limo, once again looking around.

Captain Murphy was in the driving seat with one of the men next to him. The gang sat behind them and two other men were behind in a third set of seats. It was huge, this limo.

Sally, Ben and Jamie had taken it all in. It felt safe inside, especially when they looked beyond the windows to what looked like chaos. The NYPD car attracted attention and people pulled over to let it pass and in the busier areas Murphy put his siren on, especially to excite the kids.

When they arrived at the Manhattan apartment, Sally couldn't believe her eyes. The building was so clean looking. Captain Murphy's apartment was on the top floor. It was a tall building and an elevator took them up. Even that was big and they were all able to fit in at one go.

The main door to the apartment was strong looking. Jamie whispered to Sally, 'Reinforced for safety reasons.'

Ben's eyes widened, 'Safety reasons, what does that mean?' He clutched Sally's hand.

Jamie groaned. 'That's a silly question, what does safety mean?'

Sally poked Jamie in the ribs and said, 'Please don't start on him now, this is supposed to be a holiday for us.'

Once through the strong door they were in a spacious hall. There was a table against the wall with many phones on it in different colours.

Captain Murphy was speaking quietly to the men who had accompanied them from the airport. When they left, he called them through to the next room. Sally looked about her and thought what a lovely home it was. There was a big fireplace, and placed in the middle of the room a long coffee table, around which were tub chairs with huge colourful cushions. The telly was enormous and on the light-coloured walls were brightly coloured paintings of people and shapes.

All Ben could do was stare at it all and say, 'Wow.' Jamie and Sally were awestruck.

'You like my home?' Murphy asked.

Sally said, 'Oh, we do.' Her eyes caught sight of large sliding doors which led on to a balcony.

'Take a look,' Murphy said to her. 'Walk up to the doors and they'll open automatically.'

As soon as she moved Jamie and Ben were close behind. On the balcony was the most amazing view. They were quite high up and could see for miles. It was a beautiful day. Sally looked over the edge. The tallest of the trees only came up to about a quarter of the height of the apartments.

At the sound of voices they turned. Captain Murphy called to them. 'Come on in and meet my son, Dwight.'

Sally went first with Ben close behind her. Jamie hung back a bit.

Dwight was big, like his dad. He said, 'Pleased to meet you guys.'

Jamie studied him closely. He didn't like the way he was looking at Sal. He said, 'I've seen you before. Have you been on telly?'

Dwight found this amusing. 'No such luck. I guess it was someone who looked like me.'

Ben changed the subject quickly. He could see Sally was worried that Jamie was going to say something about the scope. That's where they'd seen him. He said, 'Dwight, that's an unusual name.'

Dwight agreed. 'I guess it is to you, but I'm real proud of it. My Pop named me after a great American president. He was a war hero.'

'Your dad?' Ben asked innocently.

Dwight laughed. 'No, the President. My Pop's name is Woodrow – after a president too.'

Sally looked at him thoughtfully. 'Does that mean, if you have a son, you'll name him after a president?'

Dwight shrugged. 'Gee, I hadn't thought of that. Yeah, I guess I would.'

Murphy eased himself out of the comfort of his chair. He enjoyed listening to them. He said to the gang, 'For the rest of the day you relax. Dwight will look after you while I work out what we're having for supper.' His main reason for leaving the room was to speak privately to the professor in London. He had to let him know about the Mario guy and that the kids had arrived safely.

'Your dad's nice,' Ben said. 'Does he always do the cooking?' He was standing next to Dwight and felt very small. If only I could grow a bit bigger, he thought wistfully, I'm sure I wouldn't cough so much.

Dwight had to think hard before answering Ben's question about food. He said, 'It depends, if he's busy at work I go to get something for us at the diner. But if he's on holiday or it's his day off he spends hours in the kitchen cooking something special. It's his hobby.'

Ben really liked Dwight. He said, 'I don't have a dad. Well, I do, but I don't see him.' He could feel his cough coming on so he dashed out on to the balcony, took some deep breaths and came back in. Then he remembered the bag of goodies Lillian had given them and grabbed a bottle of juice and had a long drink. He didn't want Dwight to see him coughing.

'Are you all right, Ben?' Dwight called.

Ben felt much better and nodded.

'Gee, I'm sorry about your dad, Ben, that's really tough.'

Sally said, 'I have a dad but no mum and Jamie has neither.'

Jamie lifted his head out of one of Dwight's books and said, 'What she means is that I don't know who my parents are.'

Dwight didn't know what to say and Sally could see that. She said, 'It's not so bad, we have each other because my dad has fostered Jamie and Ben. So they live in my house – with me and Dad.'

She didn't want to go into any details about her dad's illness, it was too complicated.

Dwight said, 'What do you do at Christmas and times like that?'

'We have a super time, really cool. We have a tree and all that stuff and we give each other presents.'

Sally felt herself getting close to tears again and she didn't want that to happen. Dwight's home was like a palace compared to hers.

Ben said in a business-like way, 'I save all year for Christmas.'

'We do odd jobs,' Jamie put in, 'like delivering papers and gardening for the professor. It's okay.'

Captain Murphy called from the kitchen, 'Dwight, as a special favour you can borrow my baseball bat tomorrow – show your friends how it's played.'

Dwight shuffled his feet and didn't answer immediately.

Murphy poked his head round the door and said, 'My baseball bat, Dwight, its okay for you to use it tomorrow.' He disappeared again and they heard the front door to the apartment open and close.

Dwight said, 'That'll be Pop going to get our supper.'

There was a bit of a silence. What on earth should he do? He'd have to explain to the gang – come clean. He said in a lowered voice, 'Look, I'm sorry guys, but it won't be possible to play baseball tomorrow. I'm in a spot of trouble.'

Sally placed a finger over her lips and said to him, 'Will you excuse us for a moment, Dwight?'

'Sure, no problem.' He was confused enough about the bat, and now they were heading for the balcony and having a private talk.

Outside they huddled in a corner out of sight. Sally said, 'We know what's happened, don't we?'

Jamie and Ben agreed. Jamie said, 'But we're sworn to secrecy, Sal.'

'I know, I'm not saying we should tell him about the professor's invention.'

Ben said, 'What then?'

'We've got to tell him that the bat's safe and we know how to get it back,' Sally urged.

'You're good at that sort of thing, Sal, you do it,' Jamie said. 'We'll back you up.'

'We're agreed then?' Sally finally said.

They nodded and joined their little fingers together in understanding. With Sally leading, they went back inside. Dwight was slumped in one of the tub seats cuddling a cushion and looking into space.

The gang went up to him. Sally spoke first, 'Dwight, we have something important to tell you.'

He looked up at them and tried very hard to look happy. The gang were his guests and he felt terrible.

Jamie gave Sally a gentle nudge to continue. She said, 'We know about the bat.'

Dwight stared at them. 'You know? You can't know!'

Sally persisted. 'We do, we know all about it.'

'You couldn't.' Dwight was close to tears.

Ben said in a bold voice, 'Try us – go on.'

Dwight blew his nose and said, 'You couldn't possibly know – you were in London yesterday.'

Interrupting, Jamie said, 'There is no baseball bat because ... '

Sally said quickly, 'Because it isn't here.' She thought it a bit tough and mean of Jamie to say what he did.

Dwight looked at her for a long time, trying to work out in his mind what they were talking about.

When he did speak it was with a croak, 'Can you guys keep a secret?'

They huddled around him. At least he has us, Sally thought. If only he'd make it a bit easier for us.

At last Dwight started to explain. 'Well, it's like this. Yesterday I borrowed – no, took – Pop's baseball bat without permission and I've lost it.'

With relief Sally put her arms out and hugged him. 'You haven't lost it.'

Almost at his wits' end, Dwight said, 'I have. How would you know? You see, I wanted to impress my friends and now I've lost it.'

Ben crawled closer to him and said in a conspiratorial voice, 'We know who's got it.'

'Gee, Ben, be serious for a minute.' Despite his terrible dilemma Dwight already felt like a big brother to Ben. He was so frail looking.

Jamie was getting a bit bored with the time it was taking. He said, 'We are being serious – it was the guy with the red hat.'

What a mouthful, Sally was angry. Surely Jamie could be a bit more tactful? To make things easier for Dwight, she said as casually as she could, 'Yes, a guy with a red hat. He's got your dad's baseball bat. Do you know anyone who wears a red hat?'

Dwight said, 'Brad wears a red hat. I don't understand, what's going on here? How do you know?'

Ben put in, 'He pinched it when you weren't looking. So we can go and pinch it back.'

Dwight was confused. 'This is weird, Brad's my best friend. He wouldn't do that to me.' He gave them a strange look. 'How do you know?'

Sally said softly, 'Let's say, we have a way of seeing things other people can't.'

Bemused, Dwight said, 'Seeing things other people can't – hey, are you guys telepathic or something and you're not telling me?'

With a superior voice, Jamie said, 'Sort of.' He could see Dwight was taken with Sal and he was letting him know who was boss around here.

'Actually, it was the Man in the Moon,' Ben said with a serious face.

'That's right,' Sally laughed.

Jamie raised his eyebrows and shrugged. Before they left London they'd seen it all on the scope, the boy with the red hat. They'd told the professor and he repeated what he'd said before. 'Say you can see things other people can't, it's simple!' But it wasn't simple, they had to lie.

They heard the front door open and close again and then rattling of plates in the kitchen. Eventually, Captain Murphy appeared weighed down with a huge tray of Chinese food. 'Tuck in, kids,' he said, 'Oh, soy sauce!' He went to get it.

Ben dug into the food. With a full mouth, he said, 'We can go with you to Brad's house and get it back.'

Murphy came back with the sauce and was pleased to see they were eating heartily. But they were very quiet. He said, 'Well, the food's okay, I can see that.' He was about to comment on their unusual quietness when the phone rang. 'Don't wait for me guys, carry on,' he said. 'Not my day today.' He left the room again in a hurry.

As soon as the door was closed, Dwight said, 'This is weird, how do you know about Brad?'

They all had full mouths. Sally spluttered, 'Because we have x-ray eyes.' She grinned at him.

Dwight felt more relaxed. It made sense that Brad pinched his Pop's bat for a bit of fun. Jokingly, he said, 'You didn't answer my question, are you guys telepathic or not?'

Jamie said in a superior voice, 'Sort of.'

Sally filled her mouth with a spoonful of rice and said, 'That's right.' As she spoke small pellets of rice flew all over the table.

They all laughed, except for Dwight, who was totally bewildered.

Sally felt herself blush. 'I'd better go and clean myself up.' She'd glanced at Dwight and caught him looking at her. He said, 'You know where the bathroom is?'

She nodded and slipped out of the room quickly. To get to her bedroom she had to pass by a door that was ajar. Inside, Captain Murphy was on the phone and she couldn't help hearing. What she heard terrified her. He was speaking to the professor about a man in dark glasses who'd followed him to the Savoy when he was in London. His name was Mario and he was a spy.

Edging herself closer to the open door she tried to see inside. She wanted to know if the Captain was recording his talk with the professor. If the professor was going to tell Captain Murphy about his invention she wanted to know. All she could see inside was a room full of books and papers. This must be his study. It looked a bit like the professor's study, untidy with a large desk covered with all sorts of machines. One of them, she was sure, had to be a recorder. She'd seen this sort of thing on telly.

There were long gaps when the Captain didn't talk, so the professor must have a lot to say. Suddenly, the Captain spoke. 'I wasn't surprised at the info that came through about the fingerprints and photos. The guy has a long cop record throughout Europe. Born in the Ukraine and speaks six languages fluently.'

Sally's heart was beating fast. Any moment Jamie would come to see why she was taking so long in the bathroom.

The Captain was getting more excited about the man's name. He was sure that the man who had phoned him from London was Mario. He said, 'There's just one thing on my mind, Professor, the safety of the children. I plan to travel around with them in my NYPD car.'

At last he said goodbye and replaced the receiver. At that point, Sally squeezed her head round the door just in time to see him pressing a button on a machine that looked like a recorder. Jamie would know how to work it.

In a flash she was in the safety of her bedroom. It was so pretty and to have a bathroom as well – it was magic. For a brief moment the worry of her dad and seeing Mario in the caravan with so much money vanished.

17
The professor's place

THE PROFESSOR WAS in his hammock, listening to the birds singing, thankful that the children were safe in New York and the Mario fellow would be dealt with by the NYPD. He could hear Mrs Gannon rushing around as usual with her duster. She appeared with a mug of coffee for him.

'I haven't seen the children lately, Professor.' She put his coffee on a stool and helped him out of the hammock. The professor smiled. She could get him out of his hammock better than any of them.

He said, 'They're on a little holiday, Mrs G.'

She'd brought her own coffee out and settled herself in a seat. The professor wasn't so happy about this. No doubt he would hear about all her worries and she'd prattle on for ages.

'A little holiday, that's nice. Gone to the seaside have they? Blackpool is it?'

He could hear her slurping at her coffee. 'No, Mrs G, somewhere much more exciting than Blackpool.' He wished she'd go away and leave him in peace to think.

'More exciting than Blackpool, I don't know where you can go that's more exciting than Blackpool. We go every year, always have done.'

The professor handed her his empty mug, hoping she'd get the message. It didn't work and she remained seated.

'They've gone to New York, Mrs G.'

The professor nearly fell off his seat when she shouted out, 'New York, in America?'

Oh dear, he thought, now she'll want all the details. He said in a solemn voice, 'Yes, New York in America.' It was his own fault and he waited for the next question.

'Well I never, did they win the pools or something?'

He deliberately yawned. 'Something like that Mrs G, and they're over the moon.'

His yawn had worked. She got up and collected the mugs. It was then he remembered about his visitor.

'By the way, Mrs G, I'm expecting an important person this afternoon, from Scotland Yard ... '

He was unable to finish what he was about to say to her because Mrs Gannon looked aghast at him and went into a terrible fluster.

'Oh no, Professor, I'm sorry – I didn't mean to ... '

What on earth was wrong with the woman? He had to shout to be heard, 'My dear lady, what's the matter with you? Calm down, are you ill?' If that wasn't enough for him she started to sob.

'No, I'm not ill, Professor, but I will be if you tell the man from Scotland Yard.' She'd dropped on to the grass and was rocking back and forth, with her arms wrapped around her as if she were in pain.

'Tell the man from Scotland Yard what?' He attempted to lift her up but it was quite impossible for him.

Sobbing her heart out, she said, 'If you tell him about the m ... m ... mushrooms.'

He tried to help her up again. 'Please Mrs G, do stop crying. You don't seem to be making much sense. So will you please explain, preferably without the tears.'

'I didn't mean any harm, Professor.' She burst into a wailing sob.

Shouting above her wailing, the professor said, 'Of course you didn't, but what didn't you mean any harm about?' He continued to shout, 'Please Mrs G, stop making that terrible noise, it's important ... ' He realised she'd stopped and lowered his voice ' ... important for me to be able to hear you.'

She blew her nose very loudly. 'It, it just started in a small way.' She gazed up at him like a small child who'd been naughty.

'Yes, Mrs G, go on.'

'It was more of a hobby really and your cellar was ideal.' She was twisting and turning her handkerchief so violently that the professor was seriously worried about her. He endeavoured to keep his voice friendly and warm.

He said, 'A hobby, how nice. But what was my cellar ideal for?'

She looked at him as if he'd asked a very silly question. 'Why, growing mushrooms, of course.'

He nodded and smiled. 'Growing mushrooms?'

'Aye, that's what I said.'

The professor shrugged and said, 'Now, let me get this right. As I understand it, you are growing mushrooms in my cellar, correct?'

Mrs G gave him one of her very odd looks and said, 'Is this a cross- examination?'

The professor held his hands out and lowered them slowly, hoping it would have a calming effect. He said, 'Wonderful ... wonderful.'

Mrs G looked at him blankly. 'You didnae mind?'

'Mind?' He threw his arms in the air. 'Of course I don't mind. Why should I?'

She drew her seat closer to him, which didn't suit the professor. In a secretive voice she said, 'It's not just one or two, Professor, it's hundreds.'

'Bravo, excellent,' he shouted. 'Well done.'

Mrs Gannon was slightly taken aback and hastily added in a confidential voice, 'It's highly lucrative.'

Highly lucrative. He mulled this over in his mind. Perhaps he could start charging her for the extensive use of his phone. He said, 'Of course it would be. You deserve a medal, Mrs G – to think, a cottage industry in my cellar!'

She smiled coyly, and said, 'It started in a small way you see Professor, and I found I could sell them, so I grew more.'

He continued to indulge her. 'Of course you did, Mrs G. You would have been stupid not to.'

Much to his alarm, she broke down again and began sobbing. 'Will you ever forgive me?' She held her arms up in a begging pose. He found this embarrassing.

'Now, now, Mrs G,' he said, 'you are forgiven, but on one condition – that you make me a large plate of fried mushrooms on toast for my supper.'

This seemed to please her. She said, 'Oh, Professor, of course. You can have fried mushrooms every day if you like.'

He felt for his indigestion powders in his pocket. He said, 'Well, I don't think I want them every day, Mrs G, every other day perhaps. Now, when the children return, we won't tell them about your little business, not yet anyway.'

Mrs Gannon nodded eagerly; that suited her fine. 'Righty-ho, Professor, anything you say. Oh, by the way, what happened to that man I hit on the head? You never said.'

The professor scowled. No way was he going into details about that scoundrel. 'That man? No idea.'

Obviously she had no intention of leaving, so the professor started yawning. She said, 'What did he want with you?'

'He wanted ... he wanted.' The professor yawned again as he climbed into his hammock and immediately fell asleep.

18
New York apartment

DWIGHT WAS SITTING cuddling his Pop's baseball bat. He looked at Sally and coloured a little when she crept in. He said, 'Brad's going to have a surprise, I guess.'

Sally was relieved they'd got it back for him. And it hadn't been difficult. Brad was fast asleep. He'd left it against a tree, so it was easy for Jamie to walk in and pick it up.

Dwight said, 'I won't say anything to Pop, seems no point.'

'I agree,' Sally put in. She felt a bit uncomfortable and was sure Dwight wanted to say more. He was stroking the bat and thinking. He said, 'You know, Sally ... ' She waited, but nothing more came from him. It was very odd. She was used to Jamie coming straight out with things. Not this. She picked up one of the comics and started to read.

Dwight suddenly said, 'I think you're very pretty.'

She looked up at him in surprise and didn't know what to say. He went all quiet again, so she tidied the comics and said, 'I'd better find Jamie and Ben.'

Dwight blurted out, 'You won't laugh will you, but – will you be my girlfriend?'

All she could think of saying was, 'Girlfriend? But I have to go back to London soon.'

Dwight had gone red. 'We can write to each other, send photos. Please.'

This wasn't expected and she felt confused. He's asking me to be his girlfriend and I'm only twelve. But things are different here. Dwight is definitely more grown up than Jamie. She said self-consciously, 'Okay, I'm not very good at handwriting. But I'll ask the professor if I can borrow his computer, it can write letters. I can send emails.'

'That's great,' Dwight said eagerly, 'we've got a computer too and maybe I can visit one day.'

As soon as he said about visiting, Sally could feel herself closing up. How I hate anything like this, she thought. If only we could carry on just being friends. Why did he have to say that? She'd slid to the edge of her seat and Dwight noticed. He looked at his watch for something to do, give him time to think. It didn't take him long. He said, 'What's wrong?'

She fidgeted with the comics, pretending to be tidying them. She didn't want to say anything about her home – how it was so different from his, and how her dad had to work nights because daylight upset him. It would all sound so awful and it made her feel ashamed and she knew that was wrong. So she settled for, 'We don't have much money.'

Dwight was so relieved to hear her say something. 'Couldn't we,' he began, 'couldn't we get together anyway? About the money, it doesn't matter.'

'It does, Dwight,' she retorted. 'Your home is like a palace compared to mine.' She could feel the tears welling in her eyes and daren't look at him. She said, 'But I plan to work hard at school so I can go to college and get a good job. The professor will help me.' She kept her eyes downcast and sniffed.

'That's great,' Dwight said, full of admiration for her. 'Say, I've got an idea – come to college here.'

Now she did look up. She said hastily, 'In New York?'

Dwight jumped up. 'Sure, why not?'

He'd cornered her again and all she could think of saying was, 'I'll have to talk to the professor first and my dad – and Jamie and Ben.'

Dwight came closer and said, 'Can I kiss you?'

Sally got up from her chair quickly. She was shaking and thinking 'I don't want him to kiss me'. She said, 'I've never been kissed by a boy before.' It was said defensively and she made for the door, but Dwight was there before her, still clutching the baseball bat. The door had swung open as he took hold of her and tried to plant a kiss on her lips, but the bat came between them and he only managed a peck.

He stepped back and said, 'You're definitely my girlfriend now.' There was a twinkle in his eye. The bat had been dropped and the whole thing had been absurd, Sally thought. She was so embarrassed.

Jamie and Ben were standing in the doorway mesmerised. Jamie said angrily, using his policeman-like voice, 'Oh yes, oh yes, what have we here?'

Ben shouted out, 'Sally, you'll have a baby now.'

Jamie was furious with him and even more so with this American guy, Dwight. He wanted to punch him hard. He said to Ben, 'Twit – you can't have a baby by kissing.'

Sally screamed at them, 'Shut up, both of you.' She rushed from the room, with Dwight close on her heels.

Jamie said, 'You've upset her, bird-brain.' He picked the bat up, thinking how much he'd like to smash it against the wall.

'I don't think Dwight's good enough for her,' Ben said. He slumped in a chair. 'I thought I'd marry her one day, not him – just because he's bigger than me.'

Jamie cut in on him. 'You marry her? Now that's a joke.'

'Give over.' Ben tried to kick him but his leg wouldn't reach that far.

Jamie said, 'Come on, let's give the Captain his bat back before I break it into little pieces.'

There was a banging of doors and excited chatter when Ben and Jamie returned to the lounge with the Captain.

Murphy said, 'Where's Sally and Dwight?' He was on edge. The professor had phoned him during the night, just when he'd taken a sleeping pill. He thought he was having a bad dream and had to pinch himself to wake up. But when the professor told him about Mario's visit and offer of money for his invention, he became wide awake. He still couldn't believe that Mario had attempted to kill the professor, who was saved by Mrs Gannon knocking the guy out. Then phoning the police who didn't seem to take the incident seriously – mainly because there was no evidence as the body had disappeared and the scope had been wiped clean. He'd spent the rest of the night inserting an electronic tracking device into the heel of Dwight's sneakers. He was a worried man. Mario and his accomplice meant business. What would their next move be? He shuddered to think. The children must be protected.

He poured himself a stiff whisky, then called for Sally and Dwight. Once he'd got them together, he said brightly, 'So, what did you think of your unexpected outing to the Empire State Building today?'

Jamie said, 'Wicked, the guide said you can see for eighty miles on a clear day.'

Ben asked, 'Is the wind always big up there?'

'Oh yes,' Dwight put in. 'I saw a film on telly where a woman tried to kill herself by jumping off the top and she was saved by the wind.'

Sally looked at him in disbelief.

When Dwight saw her face, he said quickly, 'She was blown back on.'

Ben said excitedly, 'The man in the elevator said there were six thousand five hundred windows that have to be cleaned twice a month. And snow and rain fall upside down. Isn't that so?' He looked at Jamie for reassurance. Sometimes he got things wrong. It worried him and made him cough.

'Yeah, it's because of the powerful updrafts,' said Jamie loyally, 'caused by the size of the building.'

'Tell the Captain about the window cleaners.' Ben was really proud of Jamie. He was good at remembering things.

Jamie laughed as he said, 'So the window cleaners have to wash them from the bottom up because of the updrafts.'

'And the red rain, Jamie – don't forget about that.' Ben had his hands tightly clasped and it looked as if every inch of his small frame was screwed up into a bouncing ball, he was moving around so much.

Sally was amazed to see Jamie sit down next to Ben and put an arm round him. When he spoke it was as if he was telling him a story. His eyes never left Ben's face. He said, 'Sometimes the rain looks red and that's because the tower lights are used to celebrate something special ... '

Ben burst in to finish the story. '... and if the lights are on red and it's raining – that's why it's called red rain at the top.'

There was a brief moment of silence until Murphy started to clap and they all joined in. He felt humbled by the sheer honesty and trust of this little guy from London. He rubbed his hands together briskly and said, 'Well, kids, I've got more excitement for you tomorrow. You're going to spend the day at the NYPD – how about that?' He moved towards the door and said, 'I have to go out.'

He felt an emotional wreck and chided himself that a cop doesn't allow that to happen – a bit of fresh air would do the trick. 'See you all later and, Dwight, look after our guests until I get back.'

He closed the front door quietly and set off down to the burger bar to get something good for supper. He wasn't hungry, but the kids would be. When he got back he'd phone the professor to go over the details again and see if he had any idea of what to expect next.

'We always seem to be eating,' Sally said. 'I've put on weight and so have you Ben.' He hadn't heard a word she'd been saying. She turned back to Dwight and said, 'The NYPD, have you been before?'

'Sure thing, I often spend the day with Pop, its good fun.'

Ben looked up from one of his many comics and said, 'I wish I had a dad like yours.'

Dwight winked at Sally and said, 'One day, Ben, you just might have a dad like mine.'

Sally went red. She knew exactly what he was thinking and before they left for London she must make it quite clear to him that she wasn't ready to make such big decisions. I'm only twelve and I know dad would go ballistic. She looked round for Jamie and spied him on the balcony. Calling, she said, 'We're eating soon.'

He turned and beckoned to her. 'Take a look at this.'

With joy in her heart she tripped out to the balcony, ignoring Dwight deliberately. She stood close to Jamie as he pointed towards Central Park. 'It looks beautiful,' she said, 'all those trees and there's something special going on.' She pointed now to a group of young people, about their age, in fancy dress and dancing to guitars and drums. 'What fun,' she whispered. She was aware of Jamie's closeness and the feel of his arm against hers. She gave him a sideways glance. She'd never really looked at him before – he was handsome and she felt a little flutter inside.

The moment was taken from her by Dwight saying that the food was ready. 'We're eating in the dining room tonight,' he said grandly.

They were so different, Sally thought. Dwight was big and brash like his dad and – Jamie – he was gentle with her, understood about how things were with her dad. She could rely on him always to be there for her.

After supper she'd ask the Captain if they could go to Central Park for a day and perhaps Fifth Avenue and see the shops. Dad had a load of old films which she loved to watch. And one of them was 'Breakfast at Tiffany's'. Perhaps we could have breakfast at Tiffany's. She'd ask Captain Murphy.

19
New York Police Department

CAPTAIN MURPHY WAS in good spirits as he drove the children to the office with him. Joe had agreed to look after them while he attended to outstanding paperwork.

In his rear mirror, Murphy could see the police escort vehicle behind. His men had been filled in with the details of Mario and his associate, also about the professor in London and his invention and how the children were involved. They knew this was a top priority security case.

His plainclothes security guards were replaced every four hours at his Manhattan apartment, day and night. So far, Murphy felt safe and secure with the kids, and the plainclothes guys would follow them wherever they went, even to the bathroom. The kids were kept busy and were showing no sign of anxiety despite knowing the full story.

Murphy's discovery of Jamie and Sally in his study at the apartment had presented him with a bit of a problem. His untimely arrival had startled them, mainly because they were listening to recordings between himself and the professor.

Jamie had been open and honest with him. He appreciated that; it made the whole thing easier. Sally had explained about overhearing him on the phone. His door had been ajar and she'd asked Jamie to operate the recording machine as she didn't understand it. Jamie had said, 'We're glad we did, Captain Murphy. You'd have to tell us sooner or later.'

Murphy had to agree about that. It was something that had been on his mind, especially at night. Sally had requested that Ben should not be told. They would prefer to do it themselves when the whole horrible thing was over. 'If he was told now,' she'd said, 'it would start his cough just as it seems to be getting better.'

Murphy swung his vehicle into his allotted parking place at the NYPD, turned off the engine and waited for his police escort to arrive. His men were a great group to work with. They sprang from their car in good humour and immediately started a friendly conversation. They were specially chosen for the job, all being married men with kids of their own. Having escorted them into the NYPD building and delivered them to Joe, who was waiting in the reception area fully armed, they calmly went about their business.

Joe said, 'Where do you want to start, guys?' He was a jolly fellow and the gang immediately took to him and Murphy was confident, while they were under the NYPD roof, that everything would be okay. He left them to it.

Ben's eyes were huge as he studied Joe's revolver holster. It was very smart and shiny.

Sally said to Joe, 'Can we start in your office first? Captain Murphy says you're in charge of all the letters and parcels that arrive.'

'Yeah,' Jamie added, 'and you've got special machines to be able to see inside for bombs and things.'

'No problem,' Joe said. He looked up at the big clock and said, 'It's nearly time for our lunch break.

How about something to eat first? I'm famished – been on duty since six this morning.'

That suggestion was received with eagerness. The gang hadn't eaten for over four hours and that was a long time.

'Follow me,' Joe said. 'Where's Dwight today? He's always dead keen to have a day here.'

'He's doing something else,' Sally said. She didn't want to say that he'd been upset about Jamie fiddling around with his dad's recording machine and that she too had been listening in. That made her feel like a spy, and in Dwight's eyes she probably was. Luckily, Ben was absorbed in a film on television and hadn't heard anything. Captain Murphy had explained to them that Dwight had no knowledge about what lay behind their visit to New York. It was top secret and to be kept that way. Dwight had gone to his room sulking.

The café in the NYPD was amazing, there was so much food. They followed Joe in the queue with their trays. Ben insisted on having his own tray as he reckoned he'd be eating a lot. Joe was a bit dubious about that. Having four kids he knew that eyes could be bigger than tummies.

They all went for chips with burgers and baked beans. The burgers in New York were so big and even Ben, despite his empty tummy, could only manage half of his. This was followed with ice-cream, washed down with large glasses of milk.

By the time they got to Joe's office it was nearly three o'clock. Jamie was keen to see the different gadgets for tracing bombs in letters. Joe told him not to worry as the timing was perfect for them to see both outgoing and incoming mail. He said it wasn't all that different from the body checks they'd been through at the airports, 'Except,' he added, 'we use conveyor belts to carry the mail.' He roared with laughter. 'No conveyor belts for you at the airports.'

Jamie disagreed and said, 'Our luggage came through on conveyor belts.'

Ben saw the funny side of Joe's joke. He said to Jamie, 'We didn't go through the x-ray machines on a conveyor belt.'

Joe said casually to Jamie, 'You'll be able to see our police officers at work in the Operations Room.' This kid was a bit serious for one so young, he mused. His guess was that he and Dwight had fallen out. 'Just one other thing,' he added, 'no questions in the Ops Room. The guys on the computers have to be real vigilant.'

'There were sniffer dogs in London,' Ben said importantly. 'And the police walk around with guns.'

'Well,' said Joe, 'that's great – protection from dirty bomb threats.'

While they'd been talking, Sally became immersed in a 'Wanted' file. Joe didn't mind, so she carried on turning the pages. When she came to a picture of Mario she screamed out, 'That's him – that's the man who tried to kill Professor Venables.'

Joe looked over her shoulder at the mug shot. 'You sure, honey?'

'Yes.' She looked at Jamie and Ben. 'Remember? He was the phone man.'

'That's right,' Ben said, 'but he wasn't a phone man, was he Sally? We followed him to the caravan site in our village. He's a spy.'

The gang pored over the photo of Mario and there was no doubt that it was the same guy. There was a description of his height and build, which was all correct. And a note about his dark glasses.

'At the caravan,' Ben put in quickly, 'what about the other man?' He shook Sally's shoulder urgently. 'You said he had a posh voice.'

Joe said to her, 'Look at the other mugshots, perhaps you'll see that one too. Do you know his name?'

Sally nodded, 'Mario called him Frank, that's all I know about their names.'

'At the caravan,' Joe asked, 'did you get a good look at Frank?'

Sally thought for a moment and said, 'He was taller than Mario and thin. He didn't speak with a foreign voice – it was English and posh.'

'You said to me,' Ben reminded her, 'that you thought Frank was the boss.'

'Yes, that's what I felt.' Sally turned more pages hoping she'd find him.

Suddenly Jamie said, 'And they keep on changing their names to avoid being caught.'

Ben started to cough and he began to shake. He said, 'Where are they now?'

Sally had come to the end of the 'Wanted' book and shook her head. 'I didn't see Frank in this book.' She turned to Joe. 'Do you have another one?'

Joe shrugged. 'Maybe, honey. I had this one for Captain Murphy to study after Mario phoned him about being your benefactor.'

That seemed ages ago, Sally mused. So much had happened since then. What Professor Venables had said on the phone to Captain Murphy was frightening. And she longed to see her dad again. If only they had a phone at home in England. What a good thing Dwight wasn't with them today. They couldn't possibly have had this talk with Joe about the two spies. It was top secret and he must never know.

Ben's cough had eased, so Joe clapped his hands together and said, 'Well, guys, I think it's about time we took our tour of the NYPD.'

'Hooray!' cried Jamie, 'now you're talking.' Like Sally, although he'd never admit it, he was frightened too.

20
The professor's place

MRS GANNON KEPT ON popping in and out of the house to keep a check on the professor. He was expecting that young constable at any moment. The professor was working too hard, and she knew he wasn't getting his usual sleep during the day.

'Mrs G?' That was him calling now, she'd better hurry. His temper these days was anything but pleasant.

'You called, Professor?' She tried to remain calm but it was very difficult for her.

He was on the veranda dragging his infernal invention from its packaging. He said, 'A tray of tea and some of your chocolate sponge cake please. Don't forget.'

'Very well, Professor.' She took a few steps, changed her mind and went up to him.

'Didn't you hear me, Mrs G?' He carried on ripping her beautiful packaging from the contraption.

'Yes, I heard you, but I was wondering why, after everything that's happened, you see fit to bring that contraption out of its safe housing. It took me hours to do it.'

'Time, don't mention time to me Mrs G. Time is of the essence – not how much time it took to package my invention, but time to get to the children before they do.'

Mrs Gannon was baffled. She knew all about Mario and his accomplice. They were dangerous people and the professor should leave it to the police to sort out.

The click of the garden gate reminded Mrs Gannon about the tray of tea and the chocolate sponge. She flew into the house before the constable saw her.

'Good afternoon, Professor Venables.' Constable Evans looked as smart as ever, the professor thought, and he was pleased to see him again.

He pointed to one of the chairs on the veranda. 'Please sit down, Constable.' He sat, and, to the professor's consternation, removed his hat again. That meant this was just a courtesy call to have a chat – not vital information on the arresting of two spies. He was fraught with anger.

Mrs Gannon appeared with the tea tray and chocolate sponge. She proceeded to pour two cups of tea and pass round plates. This gave time for the professor to gain a degree of calmness.

'Well, Constable, and how are things going for you at the station?' He nodded his head sideways at Mrs Gannon. She got the message and disappeared into the house, only to return at speed to cut two pieces of her chocolate sponge and place the plates in front of the professor and his guest. Then she went.

Constable Evans answered the professor's question. 'Everything's fine at the station – never been quieter.'

'So, this is just a casual call then?' The professor took a bite of the chocolate sponge, relishing Mrs G's home baking.

'Yes and no,' the constable said as he filled his mouth with sponge cake. He slurped down his cup of tea before continuing. That was good, he thought. He said, 'I see you're rebuilding your invention again.'

The professor nodded, pleased that the constable had even noticed. He said, 'Is there a reason for your question?'

'Yes and no,' he repeated. His eyes rested hungrily on the cake.

What sort of answer was that, the professor wondered. Yes and no – impossible for him to work it out. No logic in it at all. Constable Evans was more interested in Mrs G's chocolate sponge. He cut a large slice and virtually dumped it on the constable's plate. Perhaps I can get more sense out of him now.

'Ah, you can read my mind,' the constable said, in a most congenial voice.

Mrs Gannon could see what was going on from the kitchen window. Not a lot by the looks of it, except they're devouring my sponge. I was looking forward to a slice myself.

The professor was going into one of his tizzies. He'd finished ripping off all the covering and, despite his anger at the constable, set about piecing it together. At least this calmed him and took his mind off stupid remarks.

'First of all, Professor, I have to apologise to you.'

Ah, at last a bit of sense was being uttered. The professor carried on working and said, 'And what are you apologising for?' This was going to be interesting. He couldn't wait.

'About my lack of understanding,' he said, 'of the circumstances surrounding your possible demise.' The constable waited for some reaction from the professor.

'I accept your apology, young man,' the professor said. 'Anything else?'

The constable took out his black notebook from his pocket. Reading it out loud, he said, 'The laboratory confirmed my initial findings – that there was absolutely no evidence to support that the man, Mario, was hit on the head with your invention. Or, indeed, that he was here at all.'

There was no point in arguing, the professor reminded himself. Waste of time. What was important was the safety of the children now it had been discovered that Mario was a spy, working for a government who would stop at nothing in order to obtain his drawings and codes.

The constable lowered his voice slightly to say, 'It is now in the hands of our special branch who deal with such matters. They are in close contact with Captain Murphy of the NYPD. His report from New York is positive at the moment.'

The professor looked at him blankly, 'Report? I haven't seen it. Captain Murphy and I speak regularly on the phone and he has assured me the children are well and safe.'

Constable Evans continued, 'I understand, so far, the report is verbal, a written report will be issued after ... '

The professor didn't let him finish. 'After those spies have got away with what they want – possibly harming the children in the process.'

The constable consulted his black book again. He said in a lowered voice, 'According to Captain Murphy, the children have a team of plainclothes security guards round the clock. This includes Captain Murphy's apartment in Manhattan and all outings. The Captain has even taken to driving them himself, accompanied by unmarked police cars, to places of interest.'

The professor stopped working on his scope and rubbed his hands over his brow. He said, 'That's very good of him. I must remember to thank him. We speak on the phone most days.'

'One other thing I have to tell you, Professor, is that your home here and you, yourself, have a team of plainclothes security guards – also round the clock.'

'How very good of you, thank you – that has taken a load off my mind.' The professor pointed to his invention. 'I have to build it here on the veranda – there's not enough room in the house.' He threw a cover over it and looked about him. 'I don't see anybody. Are they here now?'

Constable Evans smiled and said, 'Yes, but that's good isn't it? You're not supposed to see them, are you?'

The professor wiped his watering eyes and said, 'I took it upon myself to talk to Sally's father, without success. He works at night you know and sleeps during the day. Don't you think he should be kept informed?'

The constable got up and put his cap on. 'We've dealt with all of that, Professor, don't worry yourself.'

'He doesn't have a phone, you see Constable. I wanted to see him so I could arrange for one to be installed. Then his daughter, Sally, could speak to him herself, she must be so worried.'

Constable Evans sat down again and removed his cap. 'I can tell you this Professor – and I hope you'll keep it under your hat – a phone is being installed tomorrow. Oh, and another thing, so you don't have to worry further, Sally's dad also has a team of plainclothes security guards round the clock.'

'How excellent,' the professor said, 'but does Sally's dad know about the plainclothes men?'

The constable nodded soberly. 'Yes, he's a really nice chap. I know about his problem, he explained it to me. You know that Jamie and Ben are fostered?'

'Yes, Sally – such a dear child – told me all about it,' the professor said, 'and of her father's fear of daylight – how sad.'

Neither the constable nor the professor had noticed Mrs Gannon replacing the almost empty plate with a newly baked chocolate sponge in front of them. She stood at the kitchen window and watched. She'd heard everything they'd said, close to tears. Those poor kids, she wished she hadn't been so horrible to them.

The professor said to the constable, 'Have another piece of Mrs G's chocolate sponge before you go.'

21
New York apartment

SALLY AND BEN WERE busy writing a list of things they wanted to do and see in New York. The days were flying past and they had only one week left.

Ben said, 'Can we go to the subway? Dwight said he'd like to come with us.'

As far as Dwight was concerned, Sally kept quiet. He was a moody person and hadn't spoken to them since their visit to the NYPD. But it was really about how she and Jamie had listened to his dad's recording machine. They shouldn't have done it, she knew that, and she still felt guilty.

Sally gazed at Ben and said, 'Why the subway? It'll be just like our underground in London.'

Ben said, 'We can go on the subway to see where that terrible thing happened. You remember, some bad men flew big aircraft into the towers. Dwight said a special place has been built to remember it. It's got very big waterfalls and other things.'

'Okay,' Sally said. 'I want to spend a day in Central Park.' She wrote it down.

Ben said, 'The park you can see from our balcony?'

Sally nodded.

'That would be great,' Ben said, 'All sorts of things happen in there. I saw roller-skating and people with masks doing a sort of dance.'

'I'll ask Captain Murphy if we could do that tomorrow,' she said.

Ben jumped up and ran from the room, shouting, 'I'll tell Dwight. He'll want to come with us.'

'No, Ben,' – but it was too late. He'd already burst into Dwight's room with the good news.

Jamie was in the bathroom. He'd heard Ben shouting and groaned.

He didn't particularly like Dwight and they had much more fun without him. The only good thing about him was his dress sense. In the bathroom that Jamie shared with him, he was having a great time trying out Dwight's different hair lotions and deodorants. He wanted to look as good as him to impress Sal.

One of the security guards poked his head round the door. On seeing Sally, he said 'We're changing over, honey. See you tomorrow.'

Sally smiled at him. This guard was really nice. She said, 'Tomorrow, I think we're going to spend it in Central Park. Is that all right with you?'

'Okay with me, honey, I'll mention it to Captain Murphy. He might decide to have more of us on duty. It'll be a great day out. There's plenty to do and see.' He winked at her and left.

Jamie sauntered in, looking and smelling good. He deliberately walked close to Sally and said, 'Central Park tomorrow then?'

She looked up and said, 'How did you know?'

'Everyone must know,' he said, 'Ben shouting at the top of his voice to Dwight like that.'

Sally sighed. She said, 'It was Dwight that put the idea into his head. We can't leave him out.' She sniffed. 'Have you pinched some of his smellies? You've been ages in the bathroom.'

Jamie grinned. 'You like it?'

'It makes a change. All you need now is some new clothes.'

He scowled at her. 'And where do I get enough dollars to buy macho outfits like friend Dwight?'

Sally said quietly, 'Close the door.' Ever so quietly he pushed it shut, then sat close to her. She sniffed again and laughed.

'Come on, Sal, you were going to say something.' He edged away from her. Perhaps he had put too much of the stuff on.

'First of all,' she said, 'you must promise me not to say anything to Ben and especially Dwight.'

Jamie said, 'I promise.' He was getting edgy. 'Come on then.'

'You know we're in New York because of our benefactor?'

Jamie snorted. Sally had never heard him do that before. He said, 'If you mean Mario, the bad guy, yes.'

'Well, I know and this is true.' She got up and listened at the door to be sure they wouldn't be overheard. 'Joe at the NYPD told me that Mario had not only paid the money for our flight tickets but he also sent Captain Murphy a big cheque.'

'Wow, where is it?' This was big news for Jamie. 'Is it pocket money for us?'

'Joe said that the cheque was to be spent on our days out – things like that.' She paused. 'I've been thinking about it, surely it can include buying something American style to wear, or to take home?'

'What I think,' Jamie said, 'is that Mario wanted to make sure we'd be kept well out of the way, so he could get his hands on the professor's invention.'

'You're probably right. Anyway, Joe said to me he's been given the job of discharging the money, whatever that means – he's keeping an account book.'

Jamie frowned. 'Everything's so expensive in New York. Did he show you the figures?'

Sally nodded. 'It was all in American money, but he told me if it was converted to pounds its value would be one thousand pounds.'

Jamie gave a long low whistle. 'How much has been spent so far?'

'I don't know, being in dollars. I'll ask Joe next time we see him.' She rubbed the end of her nose with her little finger. 'I know one thing, Fifth Avenue is far too expensive. It will have to be one of those hypermarkets we've seen.'

Jamie gave a jig and a twirl and said, 'All right by me.'

The security guard tapped on Captain Murphy's door and went in. The Captain was engrossed in fitting something into a pair of sneakers.

He said, 'I'm going off duty now, Captain – back tomorrow.' He was close to Murphy's desk and could see clearly that he was putting a tracker device into one of the heels.

Murphy glanced up at him. 'Extra precaution,' he said. 'One or two other things have come to light and we have to be extra diligent.'

The guard nodded and said, 'The kids want to spend the day in Central Park tomorrow. I thought I'd better mention it to you.'

Murphy finished working on the heel and sat back in his chair. 'I'm glad you told me. I think we should have extra security cover. I'll arrange for that immediately. What is your planned time of departure in the morning with them?'

'I told Sally I would be consulting with you first.' He smiled ruefully and said, 'I could see from her expression that they'd like an early start.'

'In that case,' Murphy said, 'on your way out would you ask Joe to arrange an early meeting, here in my office, to discuss necessary tactics for 'Operation Lollipop'. He wrote it in his diary while speaking. 'Also ask Joe to recruit another six men.'

The guard saluted and left. Murphy immediately pressed a button and asked to speak to a surveillance officer. He said, 'I'll be in the Operations Room from ten in the morning and will need constant access to your tracking computer.'

As he finished speaking he tapped the sneaker on its heel and said, 'Make sure you do your job – I want the kids and my son home safe tomorrow night.'

Murphy rose and went to his drinks cabinet. A stiff whisky would help.

22
Central Park, New York

THE GANG AND DWIGHT were driven to one of the entrances of the park. Ben said to Sally, 'We could have walked, it's only over the road from the apartment.' Two of the guards were sitting in the back with them and two were in the front.

As nobody said anything to Ben about walking, Dwight said, 'It's very easy to get lost with all the people in the park. Pop wanted to be sure we stick together.'

Ben seemed to accept Dwight's explanation, but then he admired anything he said or did. He'd like to stay in New York with him. Then he thought of Sally and decided only if she stayed too.

The car drove into a big corrugated iron building. Jamie could see it was corrugated inside, but on the outside it had looked different. More like a large flower shop except it didn't have any windows. It was covered in colourful blooms and climbing plants. There were other NYPD vans and cars inside and loads of telephone points around the walls. It was very hot outside but inside when they climbed out of their car they started shivering. Dwight said, 'It's the air conditioning.'

Sally was becoming annoyed with him. Dwight seemed to have an answer to everything. Perhaps the Captain had told him to be like that as he wasn't with us today, she thought. She made a point of standing next to Jamie, and what she did Ben copied. This looked as if Dwight was being cut off –

which he was, and he was very much aware of it. Ben noticed after a while and went and stood by him.

Before they left the corrugated building, one of the guards had a brief talk with them. He said, 'The park is a great place for you to enjoy yourselves in.' He looked at the list in his hand. 'I see you want to go swimming and roller- skating.'

Ben clapped his hands in delight. 'Yippee,' he shouted.

The guard smiled. 'I suggest you roller-skate first. It's pretty hot out there and the swimming pool will be a good place to cool off in.' He looked at the kids' faces and said, 'Any questions before we move?'

Ben was the first to answer. The guard grinned at him. 'Yes, Ben.'

'When do we eat? I'm hungry already!'

Sally chided him quietly. 'We've only just had breakfast.'

The guard, being a father himself, saw the signs only too well. 'No problem,' he said, 'we'll get ice-cream for a starter. How does that sound?'

'Great,' Ben replied.

'Okay, gang,' the guard shouted, 'let's go.' He glanced at his colleagues, who were ready and waiting. They nodded, all hoping it was going to be a fun day to be remembered, and nothing more.

As they left the building by a back door hidden within the many bushes outside, two of the guards went ahead, followed by the gang and Dwight. Behind them, two more guards walked at a distance. To a casual onlooker, the kids looked like any other group having fun in the park. The guards, remaining at a discreet distance, were all dressed in shorts and

T-shirts, and carried haversacks containing pistols and cell phones set for instant communication with the NYPD.

Captain Murphy checked with the clock in the Operations Room. Exactly 11 o'clock. As agreed with the guards, he made the necessary connection on the computer to start the microchip in Dwight's heel. He then sent a verbal message to the guards via their minute earplugs that he had done this. He waited for the tracking device to transmit to a satellite, which would send data by phone line back to his computer. In seconds it appeared. There it was – the flashing microchip on the heel of his son. He knew exactly what they were doing, or at least guessed, as Dwight's heel was moving back and forth at great speed. The kids were roller-skating. Murphy relaxed in his chair and drank his coffee.

It was going to be a long day. Joe would take over while he took his lunch break. When he'd eaten he would go to his office and make his daily call to the professor. While the professor and Sally's dad had surveillance round the clock, it was vitally important for him to know of any unusual happening. He had no idea whether Mario and his accomplice were in New York or London. That done, he'd be back on his electronic tracking until the kids were home safely.

When you're having fun, time goes too quickly, Sally mused. They were by the swimming pool in the shade of an umbrella. The guard had been right about the sweltering heat when they were roller-skating. They swam for at least an hour, then Dwight took them to a super café and the food was a dream.

119

She noticed he had a notebook for writing down what was spent and a wallet full of dollars. It was annoying to watch him as he wrote every detail in. Jamie noticed too. He rolled nearer to Sally and she could smell the perfume of Dwight's cologne on him, or whatever he used. Jamie must have packed it in with his swimming things.

Jamie said, 'All he needs is a red box and he'd look like our Chancellor in London.'

Sally giggled at his comment and sat up. The sun was drying her skin. Captain Murphy had given her some lotion, which she handed to Jamie. She said, 'Do my back for me.'

He was only too pleased and tilted his head in a proud gesture towards Dwight before starting. But he was too busy writing up his accounts and taking an awful long time over it, Sally thought, we haven't spent that much. She casually glanced around to see if she could see their bodyguards. It was difficult to spot them, but when she did it was a great relief.

The sudden noise of the masked group dancing and singing attracted her attention. Ben woke up from a deep sleep and rubbed his eyes. 'Look,' he said, 'it's that group we saw from our balcony. They've got the masks on again.'

Jamie groaned as Sally stood up to get a better look. He was enjoying the feel of her skin.

'Let's join in,' Ben said excitedly.

'What about it, Jamie?' Sally said, as she swayed to the rhythm of the music.

'If we must,' he said. 'We'll have to pack everything up, they move pretty fast.'

Dwight had already packed his things away and was ready to leave. He said brightly, 'Big crowd they've got today.'

The masked leaders of the group were running around inviting people to join in. One of them came up to Dwight holding out a handful of the colourful masks. 'It's all free,' the guy said, 'just do what we do.'

Suddenly the guitars and drums stopped and a woman's voice spoke through a microphone. Sally wasn't sure who was male or female because of the masks. They were wearing bright colours and looked like actors dressed up as jokers.

The woman said, 'Stay with us for five minutes or five hours. Sing and dance along with us.'

Ben had his mask on already and was raring to go. Sally held him back and said, 'She's not finished talking, listen.'

The woman held a collection box up for everyone to see. She said, 'We're a group attached to the Free Church – any money you place in our boxes will go to needy kids or one of our soup kitchens. God bless you all.'

The music started again accompanied by a chant sung by a choir. Sally turned to Jamie and said, 'I'm glad we're starting slowly.' She looked down at Ben who had started to cough. The mask would be too hot for him. 'Take it off, Ben,' she said, 'no one will mind.' Ben clung on to his mask as the music and singing increased.

Murphy's security guards, keeping within the shadow of the trees, surrounded the performers as they moved. They were able to speak to each other through their hidden microphones. There were eight guards and they were able to confirm to each other that 'Operation Lollipop' was intact.

Murphy was sitting at his computer studying the flashing microchip in Dwight's heel. Its movement was irregular – sometimes fast, sometimes slow. He guessed the kids were doing something a bit more energetic. Heaven knows what in the heat outside. He checked the clock on the wall of the Operations Room. Sixteen hundred hours. Murphy breathed in deeply and murmured to himself, 'Not long to go – at sixteen thirty hours precisely my security guards will be rallying 'Operation Lollipop' together, arriving back at the apartment for seventeen hundred hours.' He noted everything in his book and waited for confirmation from his senior guard that everything was okay.

The gang and Dwight were enjoying every moment of being with the group of actors from the church. The crowds along the walkway were really appreciative and gave generously when they stopped for refreshment and passing the boxes around. Jamie didn't like being stuck in the middle, it was too hot. But they'd agreed to stick with each other. There must be over thirty of us now, he thought. More often than not the music was really cool and they did their own thing. So that was okay.

The pathway narrowed on a bend suddenly and this meant the density of the performers thinned. The gang found themselves on the edge, close to the trees. They were dancing near to a low building covered in brightly coloured blooms.

Sally and Ben were singing their heads off when the masked faces approached them. One of the faces said to Sally, 'We're going to do something special for the old folks round the corner – follow us. Keep dancing and singing.' Jamie and Dwight, who were deeply involved in the rhythm of the drums, followed automatically into the cool of the building. Dwight said, 'Thank goodness for the air conditioning.'

When the door slammed and there was total quietness, Sally knew in her heart that something was not right. The four men who stood in front of them had removed their masks. Perspiration ran down their faces. They took cans of beer out of their bags and said nothing. Jamie moved close to Sally and Ben, who was shivering. Dwight remained where he was. He was thinking, 'Pop will sort this out.'

When the men spoke, it was in a language they didn't understand. Things happened quickly. A door at the back was thrown open. Tape was roughly placed over their mouths and sacks thrown over their heads. They were pushed through the door and straight into a waiting van. Ben clung so tightly to Sally's arm that she could feel his nails cutting through her skin and blood running down. There were no seats and the floor was hard. Sally was sure she could smell someone else in the back of the van with them. The engine started and they moved slowly at first, then with increased speed. No one moved. They were terrified.

After a while they heard a movement. Whoever it was breathed heavily. The sacks were pulled from their heads and before them loomed a fat woman. The inside of the van was brightened by a skylight, its beam flickering over her ugly face as they passed beneath trees. When she moved to sit in a well-cushioned armchair she swayed with the movement of the van. Her legs and feet were swollen and her arms hung heavily at her sides. It was like watching an animal in the zoo, Ben thought. Perhaps she was a gorilla, although she wasn't covered in hair. All eyes widened as she lowered her great bulk and descended with a thump of such magnitude that it caused the van to swerve, her layers of fat drooping over the edges of the seat. She lit a cigarette and stared at them. Ben's eyes caught sight of some bottles of water in her bag. She threw him one and laughed. He couldn't drink with tape over his mouth so he tried to pull it off. The gorilla screamed and waved a stick, half rising out of her chair. A sliding hatch flew open at the front of the van and a man's face shouted at her in a foreign voice. She waved her heavy fists and grabbed at Dwight's feet for his sneakers, hurling them through the hatch. The man laughed and chucked them out of his window. Sally gasped. It was Mario. Ben started to cough.

Murphy's eyes were glued to Dwight's microchip. Something wasn't right, they'd gone off course. Wherever 'Operation Lollipop' was, there was no movement. The flashing had stilled. He snatched his mobile as soon as it rang and listened.

'Security guard six speaking, Captain. We have lost 'Operation Lollipop'. The time is sixteen thirty hours. We await your instructions.'

Murphy sent back a message, 'Return to base.' His heart was heavy as he turned back to the screen only to see that the tracking device had ceased to operate. There was no flash, only blackness.

After arranging for another officer to take over from him Murphy returned to his office and immediately poured himself a whisky.

His door flew open and Joe entered clasping an envelope. 'Same as last time,' he said, 'it was left on my desk.'

Murphy daren't say anything to Joe, but he wondered if this was an inside job. He mumbled, 'Open it and read it to me.'

'It's cut-out bits from the papers, all in capitals,' Joe said. His hands were shaking as he started to read, 'WE HAVE 'OPERATION LOLLIPOP'. STOP. GIVE US WHAT WE WANT AND WE WILL RETURN YOUR GOODS.'

Saying nothing, Murphy got up and poured himself another whisky, and one for Joe too.

23
The professor's place

'WHO ON EARTH IS ringing us at ten o'clock at night?' Mrs Gannon poked her head around the professor's study door.

'If you answer it, Mrs G, you'll find out,' the professor said. He was in a bad temper as his calculations on his scope were not making any sense at all. And it didn't help having Mrs G living in his house at the moment. He sighed, but it had been recommended by the police as they maintained Mrs G was as much at risk as the rest of them.

She picked the phone up nervously. Since the terrible business of Mario and the scope in the professor's garden, her nerves had been playing her up something dreadful. She said in a shaky voice, 'Hello, who is that?' When she heard the voice of Captain Murphy she relaxed and handed the phone over to the professor.

'He phones me every day to tell me that everything is okay,' the professor mumbled as he took the receiver. 'Good evening, Captain Murphy, what delights have the children had today?'

He sat down slowly and placed a shaking hand over his lowered forehead.

Mrs Gannon remained in the study. The Captain seemed to be talking for a long time and the professor was becoming more and more agitated. When he finally replaced the receiver, he said, 'Sit down Mrs G. The news is not good.'

She did as she was told and didn't rush him. The professor pushed his papers aside angrily as he lifted his head. Mrs Gannon was startled to see tears running down his cheeks. He wiped them away and said, 'The children have been kidnapped and the Captain has received a ransom note saying they will be released if I were to give them all the information on my invention.'

'Your invention – what's so important about it?' Mrs Gannon looked bewildered.

The professor shook his head wearily, 'It's a long story, Mrs G, and somehow I don't think you'd be interested.'

'That's not true, Professor, of course I'm interested, especially if it's put the bairns in danger.' She was about to gather up his papers, which were being blown through the French windows all over the garden, when the constable arrived.

With no smile on his face this time, the constable walked briskly towards the professor, sitting at his desk. He said in a lowered voice, 'You've heard from Captain Murphy?'

The professor nodded. He pointed to the nearest chair and whispered, 'Sit down.' He then turned to Mrs Gannon and said, 'We need tea, Mrs G, very strong, please.'

She left them, feeling totally inadequate. The professor had dismissed her in front of the constable. All she wanted to do was help.

On seeing the papers blowing round the garden the constable jumped up and retrieved as many as he could. He shouted to the professor, 'Are these your papers on the invention?'

Raising his arms in the air, the professor called back, 'It doesn't matter, leave them for the moment.'

'Leave them? I can't believe you said that, Professor.' He continued to collect as many as he could.

Mrs Gannon returned with a tray of tea and immediately called to the constable to come back in. 'I'll do that, you have your tea.' At least this way, she thought, I can be of help.

Exhausted, the constable came back in and sat at the table. He removed his hat and suddenly thought of Mrs Gannon's chocolate sponge. He could see her racing round the garden, grabbing the flimsy bits of paper. When she dragged herself back into the office he said, 'Any of your chocolate sponge in the kitchen, Mrs Gannon?'

Ignoring the constable's request, she picked up a heavy book and placed it on the papers. 'There,' she said, 'that should hold them down.' She looked pointedly at the professor and said, 'Those papers are important.' She glared at him and staggered from the room.

He didn't bother to look up or say thank you. What was the point? His calculations were not agreeing with the scope's range. His original papers were in the bank vault – the true and correct ones. All he needed was a calculation that would take the scope's range into space – false documentation that would con the spies enough to return the children.

When Mrs Gannon returned with a new chocolate sponge, the constable invited her to sit with them. The professor remained in a desolate frame of mind and took no notice.

Constable Evans was very much aware of the professor's low spirits. He had to provide statistics, plans and codes that were enough to bluff Mario and his accomplice within the next few days.

He spoke with care. 'Captain Murphy is following the appropriate investigations as this kidnapping is a federal offence.'

At last the professor seemed to come to life, 'All ports and airfields must be covered, roads too.' His clenched fist banged on his desk as he spoke.

With as much reassurance as he could muster, Constable Evans said, 'These investigations are already in operation, Professor, on both sides of the Atlantic.'

'We're talking about preservation of life,' the professor croaked in his wretchedness. 'Prompt and safe return of the children.'

Mrs Gannon remained silent. The enormity of the situation was heartbreaking – those poor dear children, what must they be going through?

'And Sally's dad, has he been informed?' The professor took hold of the constable's arm. 'I must go and see the poor man, he must be distraught.'

Two hours later Constable Evans left the professor's house with the promise to let him know of any information, however small. This was his first kidnapping case involving organised crime. The Intelligence Unit who'd taken over the investigations had included him in the project team. This was an honour for him and he hoped he'd live up to it.

He closed the white gate behind him and listened for the catch. Placing his police hat on his head, he straightened his back and strode down the hill.

24
The van

THE VAN SLOWED to a halt and the engine was turned off. It was dark, so they must be in another building. The fat woman rose, carrying a torch. She crossed to the children and ripped the tape from their faces. Ben screamed, it hurt. He grabbed his bottle of water and drank furiously, he was so thirsty. He shouted to the gorilla woman, waving his empty bottle. So she threw more bottles at them and they drank feverishly.

The back doors were flung open by different faces. Sally couldn't see Mario, but she knew it had been him driving the van. The gorilla woman pushed them out, throwing their bags after them.

Dwight hissed, 'Whoever these guys are, they might have the decency to treat us with a bit of respect.'

The gang wondered where they were. Jamie said, 'We're in a hangar.'

There were no lights on. 'How do you know that?' Sally asked.

'By its smell, all hangars have the same smell.'

They couldn't see but they heard foreign voices talking. It sounded like shouting to Jamie.

When the lights came on, Sally saw that Jamie was right. They were in a hangar and there was a white aircraft. It was quite small.

Everything happened quickly. The hangar doors were opened and they were pushed by the gorilla woman up some steps into the plane. It wasn't dark outside and Jamie searched for something he might recognise. When the gorilla woman saw his hesitation she carried him bodily into the plane and threw him down on a seat.

Sally, Dwight and Ben were already seated, gazing round at the plush inside. Their chairs were white leather and there was a thick carpet. It was like sitting in a lounge, not on an aircraft. The cockpit door was open and she could see Mario and one other man. They daren't look out of the windows, but they could feel that something was pulling the aircraft from the hangar. The gorilla's eyes hardly left them as she prepared food at a bar.

Sally desperately wanted the bathroom. Opposite the bar she could see a door. She held her hand up to be noticed. The gorilla strode over to her and said, 'Hmm?'

Sally said. 'I need the bathroom.' Her voice was trembling.

She was grabbed by the shoulder and dragged to the door. The woman kicked it open and pushed her in. Inside, it was more than a toilet. It had a shower and soft towels and nice-smelling soap. Her whole body was trembling. She sat on the toilet and relieved herself, which seemed to take ages. Then she ran water into the basin to wash herself, but the soap kept slipping from her hands on to the floor. As she dried herself the door flew open and she was dragged back to her seat.

The gorilla woman repeated the process with the others. When it came to Ben, he screamed, so Jamie went with him.

The aircraft was getting ready to take off. All the curtains had been pulled, so they couldn't see anything. It didn't make a big noise like the Jumbo from London, and when they were in the air, it hummed gently.

The gorilla pulled the curtains back so at least they were able to see the sky. Then she placed bowls of food in front of them. Ben sniffed his and said, 'What is it?'

Sally took a taste. 'It's porridge, something you like.'

Glasses of milk were put in front of them. All the food was consumed in silence. They had been hungry.

If they dared talk, the gorilla woman would wave her stick at them. They had no idea of the time. Dwight's watch had been taken and their bodies and baggage searched. Shoes had been removed. Sally thought this was because of the lovely carpet. Each of them had been given a blanket and in very little time they slept the sleep of the exhausted.

25
Captain Murphy's office

MURPHY WAS BESIDE HIMSELF with grief and worry. He'd been unable to sleep. There was no point in going to his apartment. The FBI was following every possible avenue and a Special Intelligence Unit had been set up. Airports, rail stations and roads were under constant surveillance.

He buzzed Joe's desk and got him immediately. He said, 'Anything new, Joe?' Like himself, Joe had taken no rest either.

'Sorry Captain.' He must have fallen asleep over his desk. His voice had that sound.

Murphy's phone rang and he felt almost afraid to pick it up. Joe burst into his office and said, 'Pick it up, Captain.'

He did. It was the Professor. 'Sorry to disturb your sleep, Captain Murphy.'

Sleep, what sleep? Murphy wanted to scream. He said, 'That's okay, Professor. There's nothing new – too early yet.'

Joe nudged Murphy's arm and whispered, 'The Professor's scope, remember?'

Murphy nodded. 'I've had a thought, Professor. Your scope picked up the ESB aerial disaster. If it can do that, can't it pick up where the kids are?'

Murphy thought the line had gone dead. There was no reaction.

'Forgive my hesitation, Captain,' the professor explained, 'but you don't seem to realise that the information it picked up was a coincidence.'

'How come, Professor – can it see things other people can't, or not?'

Murphy could hear him groaning.

'Yes, it can – it's taken me years of concentrated work, with dials and statistics. And when Ben was fiddling with it, my scope produced the first positive reaction to the codes he, unknowingly, entered into its memory.'

'So, you're saying, Professor, that the scope is capable of finding them?'

'Yes, that's why that wicked man Mario wants it so badly for his government – whoever they may be.'

Murphy said, 'How long will it take you Professor to complete your calculations?'

'Weeks, months, I cannot say – it depends on criteria.'

Criteria! Murphy was not a physicist or mathematician. He said, 'Like the Enigma code?'

The professor was mollified. 'You could liken it to that, yes.'

Joe handed Murphy a stiff whisky.

26
Another world

THEY WOKE WITH A START as the plane bumped on an uneven surface until it came to a standstill. Sally rubbed her eyes. Then Jamie and Ben stirred. Dwight took a bit longer. The curtains had been pulled across and they couldn't see out. The gorilla woman was snoring in her chair.

Sally dared to lift the edge of her curtain but a hand holding the stick barred her view. The gorilla woman was awake, and she stank. She was leaning over her menacingly. Why on earth didn't she have a shower? Sally's head felt muzzy and she wanted to lie back and sleep.

The gorilla plodded to the bar and made more porridge. She grinned. The sleeping draught had worked well on the kids. Soon, she'd be shot of them and the stash would keep her in vodka until the next job.

Sally stood up unsteadily and went to the door and pointed. The gorilla nodded and flapped her hand. Inside the bathroom she ran a shower and stood under it until the muzzy feeling faded.

When she returned to her chair, the blanket had vanished and a bowl of porridge lay in its place. The others had eaten theirs, and they took it in turns to use the bathroom.

Not being able to speak was upsetting. At least their chairs faced each other and they had a sort of communication with their eyes. If only the gorilla would go to the toilet, but that didn't happen. She must have gone when they were sleeping, Sally mused.

They sat for ages before anything happened and when it did, it was fast and alarming. The cockpit door opened and a voice called to the gorilla woman. Jamie had a good view. She was pulled through by a man holding a handkerchief over his nose and the door slammed.

Dwight said, 'We can speak.' He looked relieved, but Jamie shook his head and nodded to a small camera above the exit door, pointing in their direction.

Ben had to turn to see what they were on about.

Sally said out loud, 'There's nothing to say that's going to be of any use to them.'

'Are we being listened to?' Ben asked.

'We don't know, Ben,' Jamie whispered.

'I want to go home, I'm frightened,' Ben said.

'We all want to go home,' Dwight answered. 'As long as we can stay together, Ben, it'll be okay.'

They could hear raised voices coming from the cockpit. Its door was flung open and the gorilla was pushed through by the men with handkerchiefs tied round their faces. Her bag was thrown at her as the exit door opened. Steps automatically unfolded and she was shoved through.

What hit the gang most was the fiercely cold draught coming through the exit door. When they'd left New York it had been hot; wherever they were now was cold. The door remained open and they started to shiver.

It was impossible for Sally to work out if one of the men was Mario. Both faces were covered and they wore hats. They remained at the exit door waiting. Outside, it was quiet, with no usual airport noises. Now the gorilla had gone, Sally lifted the curtain from her window. Outside it was bleak and flat.

In the distance they could hear a car approaching. It stopped at the foot of the steps to the aircraft, doors opened and shut. And there was a new voice. It was a woman. She climbed into the cabin and approached them. In her arms were parkas with fur linings. When she spoke in English the children felt a brief hope of release. She said, 'Stand up, I need to measure you.'

Within minutes they were warm again and ready to leave, except for Ben, who couldn't stop shaking and coughing. The woman gave him a shrewd look, lifted his chin and felt his brow. 'Follow me,' she said. 'Soon you will be in a warm place and we must get you more suitable clothes.' She lifted Ben in her arms and they followed her down the steps into the waiting car. Its engine was running and the warmth was lovely.

The two men remained in the aircraft, preparing it for takeoff. If only, Sally thought, we were on it going back to New York and this was all a bad dream.

As she was driving, the woman said to them, 'You may call me Ron.'

'That's a man's name,' Jamie said.

She laughed. 'Everyone says that. It's my nickname, my real name is Ronnie.'

'I prefer Ronnie,' Ben said. 'That's what I'll call you.'

Ronnie glanced at him, sitting alongside her. He was underweight and needed to be built up. She smiled at him and said, 'That's all right with me, Ben, you may call me Ronnie.'

Sally, Jamie and Dwight were sitting like sardines on the back seat. All three were thinking the same thing. Ronnie's going to be good fun and they tried hard to put the gorilla woman out of their minds.

Jamie spoke quietly to Sally and Dwight. He said, 'Did you notice there was only one runway? We're cut off in a cold country, aren't we?'

The road Ronnie was driving on was a bit rough looking. Sally said, 'It's so bleak and I haven't seen one tree yet.' She gasped, 'There's the sea and look at that fog.'

Ronnie was taking this all in. She felt so sorry for these kids and hated being dragged into Mario's more devious criminal projects. He'd been lucky so far, but one day he'll be caught and she'd be visiting him in a prison somewhere.

She swerved the car off the road on to a track that led to a large wooden house. Beyond, the gang could see other buildings on a better road with cafés and small stores.

Ronnie parked the four-wheel drive in a make-do carport, next to snow equipment.

'This is your home for as long as it takes,' she said practically. 'Jump out and I'll show you around.'

Inside, it was so different. It was clean and tidy and the floors were wooden, with an occasional mat. And it was warm.

Ronnie said, 'All outside doors to this place are kept locked. So don't bother trying. Just relax and try to enjoy yourselves. I know it's terrible for you but it's up to the professor. The sooner he gives Mario what he wants, the sooner you'll be home.'

'What the f***are you talking about?' Dwight looked at her with contempt on his face.

'Dwight,' Sally shouted, 'don't talk like that.' She looked at Ronnie and said, 'I'm sorry, but Dwight doesn't know anything about the invention.'

Ronnie gave Sally a quick hug and said, 'Its okay, honey, I know. Dwight is Captain Murphy's boy.' She went over to him and said, 'Big, brash, American boy – just like your Pop.'

Dwight ignored her and carried on talking tough. 'Don't you dare bring my Pop in on this. He's a New York policeman and is highly respected.'

Ronnie roared with laughter. 'Of course he is. Enough of this, I'll show you to your room.' She paused and said, 'One room upstairs with four good beds and your own bathroom.' They followed her up. 'We keep the heating on all the time, so you won't feel cold during the night.' She turned to Sally and said, 'That's your bed.' Ronnie pointed to a corner. It had its own small dressing table, something Sally had never owned. On the bed was a duvet with a cover of brightly coloured wild flowers. She swallowed hard – the wild flowers reminded her of England.

Ronnie noticed the girl gulping back her tears. She said quickly, 'You guys, take your choice.'

Their duvet covers were plain in one colour. Ben jumped on the bed next to Sally's. He said, 'This is mine.'

Jamie and Dwight weren't worried which bed they slept in.

'One warning,' Ronnie broke in, 'you'll hear me lock your door when you go to bed and don't try climbing out of windows, you won't get far in our climate.'

She left them to get used to the idea of what they had to deal with. Later on, after they've been fed, Ronnie thought, we can watch a film or, if they prefer it, play computer games.

In the corridor, between hers and the children's room, was a bolted door. Out of habit, more than anything else, she opened it to see that everything was in working order. She checked the computers first for any messages; there were none. There were four phones of different colours on the desk with direct lines to other agents; only one was flashing. She picked it up and listened to the message. It was in code and had to be deciphered – she'd do that after the kids were in bed. Satisfied for the moment Ronnie bolted the door, unaware that Jamie was watching her every move through a crack in his door.

Casually she wandered into her own room – her sanctuary – away from the brutal facts surrounding governments and politics. She picked up a photograph framed in ebony wood. As she gazed, the image smiled back at her; it was the father of her son. She sniffed furiously and brushed away the tears. They were so alike.

When the children woke the following morning, they had no idea what time it was. Last night, they'd gone to bed when they were tired. There wasn't a clock in the house and Ronnie didn't seem to be bothered.

After they'd had their breakfast of porridge and mugs of cocoa, Ronnie announced they'd be going to the store to get clothes. 'When we've done that,' she said, 'we'll come back here for a spot of lunch, then you're going to the recreation hall to play with other kids.'

The gang exchanged bemused glances. Dwight said, 'Will they speak our language?'

Ronnie scraped the bottom of her porridge bowl and licked her spoon. She said, 'Some will and some won't. Does it matter?'

Sally stood up and started to collect the dirty dishes. She said, 'It's difficult to play games with people who don't speak your language.'

'Nonsense,' Ronnie said, 'sport is one thing that's universal. The rules are the same.'

At the sink Sally had filled a bowl with warm soapy water and began to wash up.

'Hey,' Ronnie called, 'you don't have to do that Sally. Haven't you noticed the dishwasher?'

Ronnie got up and pulled down the lid to show her. 'Stick the dirties in there.'

The gang grouped round the dishwasher to have a dekko, with the exception of Dwight, who said, 'Pop and I have one of those things in our kitchen. We never wash up.'

Sally looked intrigued. She said, 'I've never seen one of these before.'

Jamie said, 'We take it in turns to wash up – on a rota basis.'

Another world

Ben screwed his face up and asked, 'What is rota basis, Jamie?'

'Haven't you been listening, bird-brain? What I've just said, we take it in turns.'

As she piled the crocks into the dishwasher, Ronnie said, 'It doesn't matter - no more arguments please.' She hummed to herself as she wiped the table down. So, she thought, the English kids are from a not so well-off home – unlike Dwight who lives in style in New York. She was already enjoying having them around.

The woman in the store was pleased to see them. She looked like a granny, Sally thought, smiling and cuddly. She had slanting eyes like a Chinese, and dark skin. Ronnie spoke in her language but sometimes she spoke words they could all understand, like okay and hello. No time was wasted in finding clothes to fit; they were neatly laid in big drawers. Dwight took more interest and picked his own shirts and trousers. Jamie and Ben let Ronnie do it for them. When it came to Sally the cuddly lady showed her a special drawer filled with warm colourful dresses and underwear. She held dresses and jumpers up against her and said, 'Yes, yes.' When it came to her underwear she nudged Sally to choose and took her behind the counter.

After the clothing was purchased, the cuddly lady made hot drinks for them and they sat round a stove and talked. Jamie noticed that the bill was paid in dollars and it was quite a lot. Two hours later Ronnie bundled them back in the car. It had been more of a social call than a shopping spree. The same thing happened in the food store, except that it was busy, so they were in and out quickly. Everything was paid in dollars.

Ben remarked, 'We could have walked from the house.' He was pointing to it.

'Not with all this shopping,' Ronnie said. 'No time for the recreation centre I'm afraid. We'll do that tomorrow.'

When they got back, the gang were beginning to flag. Ronnie suggested they lie down while she prepared the food for later on. They didn't disagree, as they felt very tired.

Upstairs they fell asleep immediately and Ronnie took the opportunity of opening up the bolted room to check for progress.

27
The professor's place: late evening

MRS GANNON HEARD the car arrive. It was the constable with another man. The professor was in his study in front of his computer, deep in thought. She walked straight in and said, 'You've got visitors, Professor.'

'Is it the constable again, Mrs G?' He removed his spectacles and rubbed his tired eyes. The scopes calculations were driving him mad.

'It is. Where shall I put them?'

'Not in here, Mrs G. I need to get out of this room. Put them in the garden, it's a lovely evening.'

Mrs Gannon returned to the front door where they were waiting. She said, 'The Professor said to go into the garden as it's a lovely evening.' She gave a little cough and looked enquiringly at the man with the constable.

'Forgive me, Mrs Gannon, this gentleman is Sally's father, John Gray.'

They shook hands and Mrs Gannon was most impressed. Quite young to have so many children, she mused, about forty perhaps and very handsome. She felt a sudden chill run down her spine. What was she thinking? The children had been kidnapped. He was without them until ... until they were returned. She said, 'Please come in. We'll sit on the veranda and I'll make a pot of tea. Is that all right for you, Mr Gray?' He nodded and said quite simply, 'Please call me John.'

They followed her through the house but there was no sign of the professor. Perhaps he's gone to the bathroom, she thought. When she'd settled them she returned at once to the kitchen. He might be in there, but he wasn't.

While she was waiting for the kettle to boil, Mrs Gannon looked through the window to see if the visitors were okay. What she saw surprised her. The professor was with them, waving his arms and papers around, almost as if he'd won the lottery. She must get a move on, find out what on earth's happened now.

Having made a large pot of tea, her eye caught the new chocolate sponge she'd made only this evening. She got out a bigger tray to put it on. It was heavy and she had to walk with care. She could see the professor in the garden.

'Mrs G, Mrs G,' the professor called, 'you'll never guess what's happened.'

The constable and John Gray were more or less involved in the celebration themselves.

'Good news, Mrs Gannon,' the constable shouted.

John Gray stood up and took the heavy tray from her and pulled out a chair so she could join them.

'Ah,' the constable observed, 'we can celebrate with the cutting of your chocolate sponge, Mrs Gannon.' He cut four good slices and handed them around.

John Gray, being a quiet homely man, poured the tea. Mrs Gannon wanted to ask if the children had been found, but her common sense told her not to. She looked expectantly at the professor. The tea and sponge were being so well appreciated that all thought had gone from the professor's head to tell Mrs G what the good news was.

She couldn't stand it any longer and burst out, 'What good news, Professor?'

Three faces looked at her blankly. The professor's drawings and data were scattered around the veranda. He said, 'I've worked it out, Mrs G. I've discovered a way in which to bluff them, hidden within the data. It'll take months to decipher – if in fact they are able to.' He crammed the last piece of chocolate sponge in his mouth and sat back elated.

Quietly, John Gray topped up their cups. He wanted to ask what happened next. He was taking it for granted the children would be released as soon as the man Mario had the fake data. One phone call to Captain Murphy in New York should do the job. He waited.

As the moment had become sober, the constable spoke first. 'Your fake calculations, Professor, how soon can they be made available?'

'Tomorrow. I'll work all night to make them look good.' The professor looked triumphant.

'And the scope itself, it can be rebuilt by you and suitably packed for an immediate cargo flight to New York?' the constable urged.

'Indeed, it can. Mrs G will do the packing.' The professor tapped her shoulder lightly, which surprised her as he'd never done that before.

In the excitement of the moment, the constable had overlooked the reason that John Gray was with him tonight. He said, 'A phone has been installed in John's cottage, which means he's available to receive calls at any time. Just a small point, we have the phones tapped just in case of any … ' he hesitated. '… of anything we've overlooked.' He hoped he'd worded that correctly. Until the children were delivered into their hands at London Airport anything could happen. Everyone had to remain vigilant.

John cleared his throat. 'I'm pleased to meet you at last, Professor. I've heard a lot about you from the children and I want to thank you for ... '

The professor held up his hand. 'Time enough for thanks,' he said, 'when we're reunited.'

They sat in silence, breathing in the clean evening air. The garden was at its best, a mass of colour, in waiting. The ringing of the phone brought them back to reality.

'That'll be Captain Murphy,' Mrs Gannon said. 'Same time every night, I'll get it.'

The professor said, 'Bring the phone out here, Mrs G. I want everyone to hear when I tell the Captain my news.'

She returned very quickly and handed the instrument over to him. He pressed a button and said, 'You'll be able to hear everything we say to each other.'

Murphy spoke first. 'Good evening, Professor, midday here and very hot. How's it with you?'

'Perfect, Captain, a warm balmy evening here and I have some good news for you.' The professor looked around to check they could hear. When the thumbs went up he continued, 'I have succeeded in producing calculations and drawings to my satisfaction.'

There was a moment's silence at the New York end. Murphy was concerned about the sound of a definite click on his instrument, like an infiltration into his conversation with the professor. He said, 'Can I ring you back, Professor? A slight problem this end with my phone.'

The professor hesitated. A slight problem? He looked at the constable, who was busy writing a quick note on his napkin. He passed it over to the professor. It read, 'Possible phone tapping internally.'

The professor said, 'Of course.' He replaced the receiver and sat back looking totally abashed.

'We'd like to stay, if that's all right with you, Professor,' the constable said.

'Of course it's all right, I'd never dream of you leaving at such a vital moment as this.' He turned to Mrs Gannon. 'More tea, Mrs G? This might take all night.'

The constable took out an instrument from his pocket, set it on the table and switched on the professor's phone call with Murphy, before it was cut off. It was very clear and the professor heaved a sigh of relief.

'Thank goodness,' he said, 'I didn't say FAKE calculations. If we were being listened to, all they would have heard was – I have succeeded in producing calculations and drawings to my satisfaction.' He stopped talking and thought for a while, then said, 'Have you recorded everything we've ever talked about here?'

'Part of the job Professor – you can see the benefit of it. At least you know you didn't use the word FAKE.' The constable returned the instrument to his pocket.

Murphy had done a pretty thorough check of his office phone lines and had the bugging busters in. It didn't take long. His phone was being tapped. In his fury he'd ripped all phone lines from his room out of their sockets and had issued an edict saying that, until further notice, communication with him would be either written internal memos or in person. Until 'Operation Lollipop' was finalised he would use his personal special cell phone in open territory of his choosing. The time and place would remain secret.

When the telephone rang in London at two o'clock in the morning, the professor, the constable, John Gray and Mrs Gannon were ready.

'No need to go into technical details, Professor,' the constable said. 'Just straightforward facts assuring Murphy that our part of the bargain with Mario is ready.'

The telephone procedure was repeated. Murphy spoke first, 'There's been no further contact from Mario but I'm sure something will happen now, especially as I've discovered my phones were bugged in the office.'

The professor said, 'The equipment you're using to speak to me now, I presume is safe?'

'Absolutely, no way does the Judas in my camp infiltrate it. Tomorrow is another day, Professor, I'll phone at the usual time.'

Murphy had made his call from a merry-go-round in Central Park. He heaved his body off the magnificent white horse – it had felt good being a kid again. Now he'd go back to the apartment and have a double whisky.

28
Another world

THE GANG HAD a bad night with Ben – he couldn't stop coughing. Sally got water from the bathroom, which he sipped. She found an aspirin in her bag and persuaded him to take it. He didn't want to. He said it stung his throat.

'Once you've swallowed it, you'll feel better,' Sally insisted.

Jamie and Dwight were getting fed up with him, so Ben put his head under the duvet to muffle the noise he was making. 'It's not my fault,' he croaked. 'I haven't stopped shivering since we've been here.'

Eventually the aspirin did help and they were able to sleep at last. In the morning, as Ben hadn't woken, they decided not to disturb him.

Sally was relieved to hear the door being unlocked. Ronnie poked her head in and said, 'I heard all that last night. What's wrong?' She saw that Ben was in a deep sleep and beckoned them to come downstairs.

The usual porridge was standing on the range keeping warm. 'Sit down and eat while it's hot,' Ronnie said. She didn't have to persuade them. The porridge was always deliciously creamy and they were allowed to cover it with honey. Despite their bad night, the gang were more hungry than usual.

'That's the different climate,' Ronnie put in, 'we're colder here.' She stopped herself just in time. If she'd said any more she might have given their location away. Not that the kids had any way of contacting anybody.

When the toast was ready, Dwight filled his plate high. It smelt delicious. Ronnie studied his every move and Sally noticed how she smiled when he handed the plate around.

'I've got some home-made marmalade in the cupboard, Dwight,' she said. 'Will you get it out?' She was being really nice to him. Once again, she followed him with her eyes. Sally couldn't make it out.

Ronnie transferred her attention back to Jamie and Sally. She said, 'That was a bad night for Ben. Has he seen a doctor for the cough?'

Jamie spoke up for him. 'He's always been like that. When we lived in the orphanage the doctor said he'd grow out of it.'

Ronnie creased her brow and said, 'I thought you were Sally's brothers.'

Jamie shook his head. 'Sally's dad came and chose me from the orphanage. Ben and I shared a room.'

Ronnie noticed he'd said 'me'. She thought for a while before saying more. When she did she tried to be discreet. 'And Ben, he was chosen as well?'

Once again Jamie shook his head. 'Sally's dad only wanted to foster one boy, but I said to him I couldn't leave Ben behind because we'd always shared.'

Ronnie glanced at Sally. 'That was good of your dad to foster two boys.'

Sally took a last bite of toast. 'Dad always said he didn't want me to be the only child. I knew he was going to the orphanage.'

Dwight gave a broad grin and said, 'And you landed up with two brothers, Sal.'

She frowned at him. 'Yes, and it's all worked out very well. I was lonely before they arrived and that worried Dad because he works nights.'

Ronnie said, 'I'll pop up and see if Ben's awake. He'll probably be hungry.' She left the room quickly. One of the phones was bleeping in the office. It was quiet upstairs and she could see Ben through the open door, still sleeping. Quickly she unbolted the office. Mario's phone was flashing. She picked the receiver up and decoded the message. It was brief and to the point: 'Professor agreed to exchange. ETA two days – will contact further.'

Following instructions, Ronnie cleared the message immediately. Two days, she thought, I'm glad for the kids. What a relief. I'll volunteer to deliver them back to New York. That way I'll know they're safe. How she hated Mario. This would definitely be her last assignment. Then she would give herself up.

Having bolted the door, she slipped into the children's room. Ben seemed to be sleeping peacefully despite his very red cheeks. She laid a cool hand on his brow. It was hot – best to let him sleep it off. Leaving the door ajar she went to her bedroom and tidied it. As was her usual practice, she picked up the photograph in the ebony frame. Every day for the last eleven years he'd smiled at her. Very soon, she hoped, they'd meet again. Instead of putting it back on her dressing table, she opened a drawer and placed it with her undies.

Ronnie expected the children to have followed her up, but when she got downstairs they were arguing about the dishwasher. Dwight was saying one thing and Jamie was saying another.

Sally was relieved to see her. They'd cleared the table and stacked the dishwasher. It was full. She said, 'We can't agree on how to start it.'

Ronnie could see the funny side of it. 'Watch me,' she said. Very carefully she went through the motions and got them to do it. She sat at the table, leaning on her elbows with her hands cupped under her chin. Only two more days, she thought, then freedom. Her packed case had been ready for months. Mario would give her very little warning. But to her, none of that mattered any more. A gift from God had arrived on her doorstep – her son.

Sally had been pulling at her sleeve for ages. Ronnie was miles away. Jamie shouted in her ear, 'We've got a question.'

Ronnie jumped, something she hardly ever did. 'Sorry, what is it?'

Dwight took the situation over. 'Yesterday you said we're going to the recreation hall for volleyball or something.'

'Yes, that's right, we are. Get your things on.' She stopped and put a hand to her head. 'No, we can't, what about Ben? He's still sleeping.'

Sally said, 'After coughing attacks, he always sleeps it off. How long will we be?'

Ronnie said, 'Depends on how many children are waiting. Perhaps we should settle for a swim instead.'

'Only if the water's really warm,' Jamie said. 'And what do we do for swimming things?'

'That's no problem – the swimming pool hires costumes and shorts out.'

'Okay, let's go,' Dwight said excitedly.

'We can only be away for one hour, no longer,' Ronnie said with a serious voice. 'I wouldn't like Ben to wake and find no-one here.'

'Or,' Jamie suggested, 'you could leave us at the pool and collect us later.'

Ronnie nodded thoughtfully. 'I can do that, I suppose. All right, come on, let's go.' As far as she was concerned this terrible business with Mario would be over in two days – and she had every intention of the kids enjoying their kidnap as much as possible.

The pool was a lot nearer than the gang realised. In the car Sally was sitting in the front with Ronnie and she could hear Jamie say to Dwight, 'We could have walked this.'

When they arrived, Ronnie rushed them in and spoke in a foreign language to the person in charge. They were handed swimwear and towels and bands with writing on, which they didn't understand. Before leaving, Ronnie said, 'The woman will get you out after one hour. I'll come and pick you up.'

As soon as she was back in the house she checked on Ben. She tiptoed to the bed and was shocked to see he was sweating heavily. Whipping the duvet off him she raced into the bathroom to get a cool flannel. Very gently she wiped it over his body in an effort to cool him. His chest sounded awful. She dragged his pyjamas off and ran downstairs to get a bowl filled with cold water. She repeated the process over and over but he showed no sign of waking. I must get a doctor and quickly. Her fingers were shaking so badly she had difficulty in unbolting the office door. Once inside she grabbed the phone and dialled. It was answered immediately. She said, 'This is an emergency, send a doctor please, quickly – no, send an ambulance fast.' There was no need to say who she was or where to come to. They would know at the local exchange.

Not bothering to bolt the office door again she went and sat by his bed, praying that help would come in time. It was heartbreaking to sit and watch him. Without waking he cried out several times and shivered. His lips were going blue. What was she to do? Where was the doctor? Please, please hurry, she prayed. She'd left the front door unlocked for them.

Oh God, he could hardly breathe. Just once, he opened his eyes and stared at her; then he was gone again.

At the sound of a vehicle she flew downstairs. It was a woman doctor. Two ambulance men hovered in the doorway. Ronnie rushed her up. It only took a few minutes for the doctor to make a diagnosis. She called to the ambulance men who ran up with a stretcher and blankets. Very gently they swathed his poor little body in a cotton sheet and lifted him on to the stretcher, covering him with the blankets. Within moments they departed for the local hospital.

Two hours had gone by before Ronnie remembered the children. Ben had been taken into an emergency room and she hadn't seen the doctor or nursing staff since. She must go to the swimming pool and collect them and she'd have to walk. Not far, but too far she thought. Ben needs us. I must go and get them, bring them to him. It might help hearing their voices. She ran past the confused receptionist without a word, out of the door and down the road.

They were waiting for her with the attendant. She was locking up for the night and was alarmed to see Ronnie in such a state. Instinctively, Sally knew something had happened to Ben. No words were necessary. They followed her, as fast as their legs could carry them.

As they ran into the reception area, Ronnie caught sight of the doctor leaving the emergency room. Gasping for breath she called to her. 'Doctor – Ben – how is he?'

Sally, Jamie and Dwight crowded round her. 'We want to see him,' Sally pleaded.

Although the doctor had the same dark skin and eyes as the children in the swimming pool, she could speak English. Her eyes were sad when she said, 'Please, come into my office.' She held out a hand to Sally. 'This way, it is easier to talk there.'

It was a small room with a sofa and one armchair. The doctor sat at her desk. Ronnie took the armchair. Sally, Jamie and Dwight squeezed onto the sofa. Their eyes penetrated the doctor's small frame.

It was not good news she had for them and looking at the children made it so much harder.

Ronnie recognised the signs. Family were very important to the Inupiat people and many of them were proud Christians who loved and protected their children from life's cruel intrusions.

As she explained, her voice was filled with warmth and friendship. She rose from her desk and knelt on the floor in front of them, taking Sally's hands in her own. She said softly, 'We have made Ben, your little brother, as comfortable as we can.' She didn't rush. A jar of sweet smelling balm lay on a low table near to her. As she spoke, she dipped her slender fingers into it, spreading the balm on Sally's hands and arms, massaging gently.

Jamie and Dwight felt the same as Sally. The beautiful doctor was almost crooning to them and they felt at ease with themselves. 'Soon,' she said, 'I will take you to Ben and you may talk to him. He'll hear you. He might make a little movement. Tell him about your day. What you ate for breakfast – but don't push him – Ben is a very sick little boy. Give him time.'

When the doctor rose from her kneeling position, Ronnie wondered if the children felt the same way as she did. How could she explain it? A deep sense of calm, she thought.

Sally brushed her cheeks with the back of her hand and breathed in the balm. She felt strong and was ready to see Ben. She looked at Jamie and Dwight. They too were ready, and so was Ronnie.

With arms around each other, Sally and Jamie followed the doctor. Ronnie wanted to put an arm around Dwight's shoulders and when he looked up at her, his face was full of joy. That was enough for her – my son loves me. Before entering Ben's room, Dwight slipped his hand into Ronnie's.

The room was a glow of colour from sweet smelling candles. Ben lay quite still. He looked very small in the middle of the hospital bed. A nurse sat quietly in a corner at a small desk, writing. Every now and again she would get up and check Ben's pulse, raise his head and wet his lips with a small sponge. There was a monitor and he was attached to so many lines.

There was only one chair, which was by the bed and close to all the bits and pieces. Sally wasn't sure how close they should get to Ben.

Ronnie slipped over to the nurse to ask how close the children were allowed to be. She didn't speak English but immediately went to Sally, pointing to the seat and gesturing her to use it.

Ronnie remained in the background as Jamie and Dwight moved to stand behind Sally. When the nurse saw this, she took the boys by the hand and walked them round to the other side of the bed.

Before returning to her chair, she demonstrated to Sally that it was all right to hold Ben's hand.

The room was so peaceful. If they spoke to each other it was in whispers. When Sally took Ben's hand it was warm. She wondered if she should hold his hand as she'd normally do, but changed her mind and slipped a cupped hand beneath his. He'd like it like this, she thought, and if he moves even a finger, I'll be able to feel it and do the same to him.

She leaned closer to him and spoke softly about what they'd been doing today. 'Jamie and Dwight are here and Ronnie.' She looked round the room for Ronnie but she wasn't there.

Jamie whispered across the bed to her. 'Ronnie's gone home, she'll be back soon.'

Before leaving the hospital, Ronnie asked at the reception if she could have a quick word with the doctor. She was taken to her office and asked to wait. Very soon she appeared. She said, 'I was going to speak with you before I leave for the night.'

'I won't keep you long,' Ronnie said. She didn't want to have to ask the question that was in her mind. She said, 'Will Ben recover?'

The doctor sat next to her on the sofa. 'He's very ill at the moment. Ben is frail. His lungs are badly affected. Everything is being done to help him. With rest, perhaps tomorrow we will see an improvement.'

Ronnie nodded in understanding. She said, 'He's not mine, you see.' How could she explain that Ben had been kidnapped along with the others? The whole thing was absurd.

The doctor placed her hand over Ronnie's and said, 'I see your mind is in torment. If he's not yours, it is your responsibility to tell his family. If the situation is worse than that – you should inform the police.'

Inform the police. Was she that transparent? Perhaps the doctor knows something – maybe in his sleep Ben had said something?

The doctor rose and said, 'I must go to my family now. It has been a long day. I'll see you tomorrow.'

She turned at the door and said, 'If it is of any help, you know I am subject to the Hippocratic Oath to respect privacy at all times.' She briefly hesitated hoping that Ronnie would open up her heart to her. When she saw the drooped head she quietly closed the door behind her.

Ronnie returned to Ben's room. The children were talking amongst themselves and Jamie was taking his turn to hold Ben's hand. She moved closer to the bed. Ben looked so comfortable. She touched his hand briefly. It was pleasantly warm. She said to the children, 'I think we should leave now. We'll be tiring Ben out!'

Jamie and Dwight nodded and waited for Sally to move. She said, 'No, I'm staying with Ben. I don't want him to feel lonely.'

Ronnie said, 'I see your point, Sally, but come home and have something to eat. You can come back later to say goodnight.'

'I'm not hungry. No, I'll stay with him. You go. Perhaps the nurse can get me a sandwich and a glass of milk. That's all I want.' Sally slipped her hand under Ben's again.

Jamie said, 'How long are you staying here, Sal?'

She said, 'For as long as it takes. If you come back later, would you bring his comics? I can read to him. He'll like that.' Ronnie saw no point in pursuing this conversation. Sally had made up her mind. Before leaving she spoke to the nurse about a sandwich and milk. She smiled and left the room to get them.

Ronnie, Jamie and Dwight returned to the house, hardly speaking a word. What a day it had been. Ronnie stoked the range and suggested they have something quick to eat. She said, 'How about cheese on toast?' The boys nodded and wandered upstairs to get out of their sticky swimming things.

Dwight pulled at Jamie's arm suddenly. 'Look.' He was pointing to the office door. It was wide open. He said, 'Ronnie must've forgotten to bolt it.'

They were in there like a flash. It had no windows and Jamie couldn't find the light switch. Dwight knocked over a small table; the noise resounded through the house.

'Now you've done it,' Jamie said. He'd found the switch and saw it was nothing serious. 'Do you think she heard?'

'No, she would have called if she had.' Dwight was already checking the computers and studying the different telephones. He knew a lot about equipment like this from seeing his Pop and Joe using it at work. Every button he pressed for recorded messages was in a foreign language. That was bad luck.

Jamie said, 'We're wasting our time. Come on, let's get out of here.'

They did, just in time. Ronnie came upstairs to tell them the cheese on toast was ready. She noticed the door and swore. It was soon bolted.

Later in the evening Jamie gathered Ben's comics together. Dwight had gone to bed and was already sleeping. He said to Ronnie, 'I'll take these along to Sal and I might stay with her, if she wants me to.'

Ronnie was clearing the table and stacking the dishwasher. She said, 'I won't come with you, Jamie. Do you remember how to get there?' Jamie nodded. She said, 'It's cold outside, wrap up well.'

When Jamie reached the hospital the front door was closed and locked. But the lights were on inside, so he banged heavily with his fist. The reception girl he'd seen earlier unlocked the door and let him in. Luckily, she recognised him and indicated for him to go through.

He tapped gently on the door of Ben's room and the same nurse let him in. It looked to him as though Sally hadn't moved. Her hand was cupping Ben's and the tray of food and drink by her side hadn't been touched.

'I've brought the comics, Sal. How is he?' Jamie could see for himself that nothing had changed.

Briefly she took her hand away from Ben's and pulled Jamie closer. She whispered, 'I've been telling him his favourite stories and once I felt his fingers moving, so I'm sure he knows I'm here, Jamie.'

He gave her arm a playful punch and said, 'Of course he knows, he's just having you on. He loves your stories.'

Jamie laid the comics on the counterpane. He said, 'Ronnie wants you to come back with me, Sal. She said you'll be tired and you need your sleep to read all day to him tomorrow.'

Sally shook her head. 'No, tell Ronnie I want to stay here with Ben. Now I've got the comics he'll be really pleased. You've brought his favourite ones, thanks Jamie.'

He felt his eyes smarting when she said, 'Give him a little kiss, Jamie, before you go.'

With an effort he picked his way through all the wires attached to Ben. He glanced nervously at the nurse. She was watching him and nodded for him to go ahead. Sally held him as he leaned over and planted a kiss on Ben's cheek.

She said, 'Thanks Jamie,' and placed her cupped hand underneath Ben's again.

Jamie knew there was nothing he could do to persuade her away, so he slipped quietly from the room.

In the early hours of the morning Ben died. Sally had read his comics to him on and off for most of the night; then in total exhaustion she had fallen asleep, still holding his hand, her head only inches from his.

29
Captain Murphy's apartment

ON SUNDAYS Murphy told people not to phone unless it was an emergency. He'd better answer it. Maybe it was the professor with further problems about the packaging of the scope. It had been agreed with Mario that the switch would be made the following day, at a point which remained a secret until he heard back.

The children were due back first and Murphy needed to see evidence of that before the swap took place. Sally's dad and the police constable were on a flight at this very moment with the scope and secret papers. They would be met at the airport and escorted by a team of bodyguards.

Murphy stretched out his arm and picked up his mobile. He hesitated when he heard the woman's voice at the other end.

Ronnie said hello again. She knew it was going to be an unbelievable shock to her husband. She said, 'Woodrow, it's Ronnie, the wife you never divorced!' She waited, then said, 'Had you forgotten me?'

He spoke. 'No, I've not forgotten, Ronnie. Why are you phoning me after eleven years – out of the blue?'

She said urgently, 'It's a long story and you can't leave New York to come to me – when you hear what I have to say.'

Murphy took a deep breath and said, 'I'm listening.'

Ronnie looked at Dwight and Jamie, as they too were listening. She'd said they'd understand better that way. It would be like a story, only this one was true.

She said, 'After Dwight was born, twelve years ago – his first birthday party – Joe was there. That's when it all started.'

Murphy recoiled when she said Joe. He thought they were just good friends, but it turned out to be more than that. 'Go on, honey,' he said.

It was such a relief when he said honey, just like old times. She became serious. She talked quickly, occasionally falling over her words.

'Joe is a double agent … he and Mario and I can give you more names. I'm one of them – we work together for other governments.' Murphy could hear her heavy breathing and gasps. 'You must arrest Joe now, today, Woodrow. Don't give him time to speak to Mario.'

Murphy was recording her admission. It would have to be used in evidence.

She told him about the kidnapping in Central Park, the flight to Alaska and her shock at discovering that Dwight, her son, was one of the children. She pleaded with him to understand her feelings when he saw her. How she'd cared for the children and given them a good time, until yesterday. She could hardly speak for sobbing at this point when she said, 'Last night, Ben died – in hospital.'

Captain Murphy took over. He said, 'Have you told Mario of Ben's death?'

The whole scenario had changed. There would be no swap and the children must be returned to New York. He would fly out and collect them. He told her that, and she would have to be with them.

'One last question, Ronnie, where is Mario now?' Murphy knew there would be no easy answer. She said, 'I don't know, please believe me Woodrow, all contact is done through coded messages.' There was a long pause; then she said, 'I know that Mario has plainclothes armed men organised for the pick-up at New York airport.'

Abruptly, Murphy asked her to put the phone down and added that he was on his way over. He turned off the recording machine. Already he had his priority list in his mind. First, a call to his superior at the NYPD, informing him of Joe's involvement in the kidnapping and the pick-up at the airport. Next, a text message to Sally's dad and the police constable on their aircraft, and personnel at the New York airport, for Security to hold all cargo addressed to him. One personal call to the main airport in Alaska – he knew the security guys there well – to provide the necessary protection for Ronnie and the three children on their journey from the North Slope to Anchorage. Lastly, he would phone Ronnie back with the information about the time and the airport where he would be picking her and the children up.

He decided not to let the professor know about the changed circumstances at this point.

30
Ben

AS SOON AS RONNIE had put down the receiver the questions came fast and furious from Dwight and Jamie.

'We didn't know Ben had died,' they both shouted at her. 'You should have woken us, we could have been there for Sal.' Tears were rolling down Jamie's face. He raced round the kitchen banging and kicking anything he came into contact with. Ronnie didn't try to stop him. This was Jamie's way of dealing with the loss. When, at last, he fell into a chair and slumped across the table, with his head in his arms, Dwight sat next to him. He put an arm round his hunched back and said, 'Gee, I'm sorry about Ben. He was a great little guy – I'd grown real fond of him.'

Jamie raised his head. His nose was running and his face was dripping. Ronnie handed him a large handkerchief. He gulped as he spoke. 'We were always together, Ben and me, at the foster homes. I was his big brother from the start.' He laughed hysterically as he said, 'I was horrible to him sometimes, but I didn't mean it and Ben knew that.'

Dwight said quietly, 'We know, Jamie, you were just having a bit of brotherly fun. Ben liked it, I guess.'

'I called him bird-brain, didn't I? But I didn't mean it horribly – it was sort of trying to get him to think a bit more, before he said something.' Jamie went to the sink, turned the cold water tap on hard and stuck his head under it.

Dwight moved to stop him but Ronnie held him back. 'Leave him be,' she murmured. He turned to her with lowered eyes. He couldn't look at her. He said, 'When I saw the picture of Pop and me in your room, I guessed. He's got the same one in his room in New York.'

Ronnie went to him. At last she was able to put her arms around her son and give him a big hug.

Dwight pushed her from him and said, 'You're a spy, aren't you Mom? What will they do to you when we get back to New York?' He was able to look her straight in the eyes now. Jamie had turned the tap off and was drying his head. He stood beside Dwight, unable to believe what he was hearing.

Both boys were staring at her with hatred in their eyes. She wanted to scream at them but she daren't. They were waiting for an explanation. She lowered herself to the floor and leaned back against the warmth of the range. It needed stoking but she hadn't the strength. They were towering over her, like a couple of gangsters, arms at their sides ready to fire.

Tears were stinging the back of her eyes, so she closed them. All she could say was, 'I'm so sorry.'

Jamie went to grab at her hair, pull it out if necessary. He bawled at her, 'You killed Ben, you did. You're wicked, you're a spy ... '

Dwight held Jamie back with an iron grip and shouted, 'No, Jamie, we can't do anything. Pop's on his way, he'll know what to do.' He looked down sadly at the woman on the floor and said in a stern voice, 'Get up Ronnie, we have to go to the hospital for Sally – and Ben.' He couldn't call her Mom – this woman would never be his mom, not now.

Sally was in the doctor's room waiting for them. When the door opened she rushed into Jamie's arms. Clinging to each other, they cried. Ronnie remained in the doorway. She felt like an alien.

When the doctor appeared she closed the door and asked them to sit. She had a luggage bag and was dressed in clothes for travelling. This time she sat behind her desk and spoke softly in a businesslike manner.

She said, 'I've had a phone call from Captain Murphy in New York.' She looked towards Dwight and smiled. 'He explained everything.' The door opened quietly and two policemen came in. They went straight to Ronnie and handcuffed her.

Ronnie hissed, 'Do you have to do this in front of my son? Couldn't it have waited?'

'I'm sorry,' the doctor said. 'You will be travelling to New York with your bodyguards. The children and I will break our journey at Juneau. There, we will give Ben a Christian funeral. Sally and I have had a long talk with her father, John Gray. Ben will be cremated and Sally will be presented with an ornamental box containing his ashes to take home to England.'

New York Airport: two days later

Murphy waited anxiously in the well-protected special lounge. He was dressed in full NYPD uniform. Ronnie would arrive first. His stomach was churning. Waiting for a wife he hadn't seen for eleven years was terrifying. He would read her her rights and then she would be driven to a women's prison. That was all. It would be brief and quick. Behind him stood two FBI criminal investigation officers, who would take over from him.

Next to arrive would be Sally's dad, John Gray, accompanied by a British police constable. Their arrival was planned to coincide with the kids flying in from Anchorage. He would see his son again and a warmth ran through him – soon drained by the possibility of losing his job because of being married to a spy. Ahead of him lay months of court trials and tabloid lies.

The door opened and a very pale Ronnie, handcuffed, stood in front of him, bodyguards either side of her. She hadn't changed. He smiled briefly then read her her rights. No further words or eye contact passed between them. She was escorted from the room, weak and paralysed with fear at what the future held for her. She swayed at the door as Woodrow's photo flashed through her mind.

Murphy couldn't control his shaking legs. He sat down and lit a cigarette. Someone handed him a cup of strong coffee.

Moments later, the door opened again and John Gray, with Constable Evans, strode in. They shook hands and introduced themselves, then drank some coffee. Murphy's shaking eased.

The timing by the airport police was spot on. The children flew through the lounge doors, Dwight straight into his arms, followed by Jamie and Sally into their dad's outstretched hands.

There was so much to talk about. Tonight, Murphy thought, we'll eat and listen and if they don't want to talk, what the hell – they were back!

Murphy's NYPD car was waiting discreetly beyond a private door. The small procession made their way to the safety of the limo, Sally first, clutching Ben's ashes in the ornamental box.

London Airport: one week later

Murphy had arranged for a flight to suit not the journalists but John Gray's daylight phobia. The kidnapping story was on every front page.

When they alighted from the aircraft in London, an extra long limo was waiting on the tarmac. Jamie and Sally were over the moon to see Professor Venables and Mrs Gannon inside. The constable and John Gray were relieved; it would ease the sadness of the homecoming without Ben.

The professor gently tapped the ornamental box that Sally was hugging. It was hard for him to hold back his tears. With a choking voice, he said, 'Welcome back children. Mrs G and I are looking forward to hearing your news.'

'We know it. It's in the newspapers,' Mrs Gannon said, 'they don't want to talk about that now.'

Jamie and Sally looked at each other. Oh dear, they were still arguing. But it was so good to see them again.

The limo was wicked inside. They sat on deep cushioned seats around a long low table. Sally placed Ben's ashes on it next to a tall bottle and glasses.

Ben

The professor turned to the constable. 'If you wouldn't mind, Constable, opening the bottle for us. I think we all deserve a glass of champagne.'

'And don't forget my chocolate sponge, Professor,' Mrs Gannon added.

'I've never had champagne before,' Jamie said.

As Mrs Gannon took out two of her sponge cakes from a box, the professor said, 'Well, there's always a first time. Isn't there, Sally?' He winked at her. She'd never seen him do that before.

'Yes,' Sally said. She laid a hand on the ornamental box. 'Ben would have liked it, I know he would.'

The professor smiled as she caressed the box. But his heart was full of concern for this young girl. She was in trauma. And he must work out a plan to help her.

The constable handed round the half-filled glasses.

John said, 'I'd like to propose a toast.'

Sally jumped up and said, 'Just a minute, Dad.' She took another glass and put a mouthful of champagne into it. Then she placed it on Ben's box. 'Okay, we're ready now, Dad.'

He planted a kiss on his daughter's forehead and said, 'To Ben – God bless you, lad – it's good to have you back.'

31
The professor's place

JOHN GRAY REMAINED SEATED as the professor and Mrs Gannon got out of the limo at the professor's house. He said, 'We won't come in – Sally and Jamie need their beds and the supermarket are expecting me in tonight.'

Constable Evans received this bit of news with reservation. He said, 'If you don't mind my saying, Mr Gray, I don't think it's advisable – after all the newspaper coverage you've had – that you go back to work so quickly.'

'I need the money, Constable. The plainclothes policeman will be with me as usual, I hope?'

John looked wretchedly tired, the professor thought. He said, 'I agree with the constable, John. Much better to stay with Sally and Jamie tonight – we can talk tomorrow.'

'The professor's right, Mr Gray, I'll come back with you to your house.' Constable Evans was concerned for their welfare. There had been no sign of Mario or his men in New York. Everyone had to remain vigilant. The scoundrel was probably in London at this very moment.

'All the usual bodyguards and plainclothes men are covering both our houses I hope, Constable,' the professor urged.

'Yes, sir,' Evans retorted. He was badly in need of some sleep himself. He said, 'Right, Mr Gray, no work for you tonight.' He remained in the limo. As they moved off he wound down a window and called to the professor, 'We'll see you tomorrow.'

Next morning

Neither the professor nor Mrs Gannon got much sleep that night. Soon after nine, Jamie walked through the gate, followed by Constable Evans.

Jamie said, 'Sally and her dad are still sleeping. I'm worried about her.'

'Come in, boy.' The professor pulled him inside, but not before having a good look around the garden and outside of the house to make sure they were safe. The usual police cars and camper vans were in sight so he closed and bolted the door.

Constable Evans said, 'There's no need for that, Professor. You're being well protected.'

The professor ignored his remarks and walked through to the lounge. Jamie followed with Mrs Gannon in tow carrying a tray with mugs of tea and toast.

'Don't suppose you've eaten this morning,' she said, looking at Jamie. 'Help yourself and don't spill any of my marmalade or jam on the carpet.' She turned to Constable Evans and said, 'You help yourself too, I've got other things to do.' She made a quick exit.

The professor shrugged. 'She's in a bit of a bad mood this morning.' He turned to Jamie, 'About Sally, why are you worried?'

Jamie had a mouthful of toast and jam and was unable to speak. He felt so hungry. The professor handed him a mug of tea. That did the trick. He gulped it down and said, 'It's Ben's ashes – she takes the box everywhere with her, even to the bathroom and she sleeps with it.'

Both the professor and the constable sat for a while pondering on what Jamie had said.

The professor broke the silence. 'She's still grieving, Jamie. But I do agree with you, it is a bit extreme to be carrying the box everywhere with her.'

'The kid's in trauma,' Constable Evans said knowledgeably. 'I've seen similar behaviour patterns before. I suggest we give it a week and if she's still holding on to Ben's ashes after that, I can speak to Miss Turner. If that's what you want me to do.'

'Ah, Miss Turner,' the professor said. 'I met her briefly before the New York trip. From Social Services isn't she?'

'Yes, sir.' The constable was about to say something to Jamie when the telephone rang. Mrs Gannon had picked it up in the kitchen and was shouting down the receiver, 'The line's not so good this morning, Captain Murphy, hang on, I'll get him for you.'

She ran into the lounge holding the instrument and threw it into the professor's lap.

'Thank you, Mrs G.' It's those damn mushrooms, he thought, they needed so much care and it was getting her down. He would speak to her about an idea he had – later. 'Good morning, Captain Murphy. Yes, thank you, everything is fine here. Both our houses are being well protected by our excellent police force.'

Murphy sensed things weren't as good as the professor was making out. He said, 'Dwight is still sleeping. It was one hell of an experience the kids had to deal with. There's bound to be repercussions.'

The professor nodded at the phone. 'Yes, there will be repercussions, as you say. Jamie and the constable are with me now. We've received bags of mail through the post, at both houses, everybody has been so kind.'

Murphy tapped his fingers on his desk. He said, 'The tabloids here are full of it – so you'll know that Ronnie is my wife and Dwight's mom?'

'Yes, our papers are plastered with it – how very sad for your son to learn about his mother in such a cruel way.'

Murphy took a mouthful of whisky. Already he was feeling dragged down by the whole horrible business. 'When things calm down,' he said, 'Dwight and I would like to fly over for a visit.'

'What a good idea,' the professor said enthusiastically. 'I have plenty of spare rooms here. You'd get no peace in a hotel. The paparazzi would be on to you in a flash.'

'Thanks for that, Professor. It'll give Dwight something to look forward to. He's pretty confused at the moment.'

When eventually he put the phone down, the professor sat for a while staring into space. Mrs Gannon clicked her fingers in front of his face. She said, 'Are you with us Professor? I want the phone if you've finished with it.'

He blinked at her. 'Ah, Mrs G, don't run off yet. I want to discuss an idea I've got – in connection with your mushrooms.'

'I'm not running off anywhere, I'm staying here if you remember, Professor, being protected like yourself.' She flopped on the couch next to Jamie.

'Well, what about my mushrooms? I thought it was supposed to be a secret.'

Jamie said casually, 'We know about the mushrooms.'

The professor gave him a quizzical look. 'Oh? And how did you know?'

Jamie didn't answer immediately and when he did, his voice was subdued. He said, 'Ben spied on her.'

Constable Evans said jokingly, 'A bit of detective work, eh?'

Jamie turned to Mrs Gannon and said, 'I'm sorry, Ben didn't mean any harm. He saw you going down to the cellar and locking the door each time.'

The professor rubbed his hands together and said, 'Well, it's out in the open now and all is forgiven, isn't it Mrs G?'

Jamie said, 'So you don't mind then?'

'Mind? Of course not. In fact, when Mrs G confessed to me, I insisted on a conducted tour of her little venture. I hadn't been down in that cellar for years.' The professor's heart had lifted. He said, 'Ideal place to grow mushrooms and it needs a specialist.' He looked at Mrs G encouragingly.

She giggled self-consciously, 'Me, a specialist? – Never.' She moved closer to Jamie on the couch and said, 'When I was about your age, I spent a lot of time with an uncle who grew mushrooms. That's how I learned all the secrets, just by watching.'

For a wonderful moment all of their sadness about Ben and the kidnapping seemed to fade. Constable Evans helped himself to some chocolate sponge and relaxed into his chair.

The professor rattled on excitedly about his plans for the mushroom business. 'I have worked out a sort of business deal,' he said, 'and of course you'll be paid handsome pocket money for your work. What do you think?'

Jamie looked at him blankly. 'You want Sally and me to be in the mushroom business?'

'Yes, of course. Who else would I be talking about?' He gave Mrs Gannon an odd look.

She shrugged and said, 'You'd only be down there for a couple of hours after school and weekends.'

Jamie said, 'I wish Sally was with us. I can't speak for her at the moment. But I'd be really interested.'

'Good, that's settled then. I know you won't regret it.' As the professor rose from his chair, Jamie said, 'What about the scope?'

The professor sat down again and said, 'Didn't you know, Jamie? My invention and all of my papers have been handed over to the appropriate police department.'

Jamie's question had put them back into the reality of the moment. The room fell quiet and their faces became haunted masks. Even Constable Evans' heart dropped like a stone. He said, 'I'd better be off.' He glanced at Jamie. 'Do you want a lift to your home, lad, or are you staying with the professor?'

Jamie rubbed his eyes and yawned. He said, 'I'll stay here. There's nothing for me to do at home.'

The constable patted his shoulder. 'I'll call in tomorrow about the same time, if that's all right with you, Professor.'

'Of course.' He walked with the constable as far as the gate, checked that the surveillance chaps were doing their duty, then climbed into his hammock. He fell asleep immediately.

Indoors, Jamie had curled up on the couch, and Mrs Gannon was stretched out in an armchair, also asleep.

32
Next day: John Gray's cottage

JOHN CHECKED SALLY'S room. She hadn't stirred and Ben's ashes lay alongside her. One of her arms lay over the box. It couldn't be comfortable for her. He wondered if he should move it and was about to do so when the doorbell rang. He took his dark glasses from the pocket of his dressing gown and put them on. It would be the postman, Phil. They'd been at school together and had stayed good friends. All the curtains remained pulled. They were never opened and Phil never commented on his phobia. John opened the door just enough to be handed any letters.

'Morning, John. Special delivery this morning from New York, addressed to Sally. She'll have to sign for it.'

John stood behind the door and told Phil to come in. When it was closed and the daylight shut out he said, 'She's still asleep, Phil. I don't want to disturb her.'

Phil rubbed his chin and said, 'Okay, mate, seeing as things are a bit dicey for you at the moment. It's not as if I don't know you, is it?'

John signed. He said, 'Have we got the usual mail bags today?'

''Fraid so, much bigger, a special van will be coming with it.' Phil sniffed. 'Fresh coffee is it?'

John grinned at his old friend. 'Come on through to the kitchen.'

'Another hot day out there,' Phil said. 'I've been thinking about all this mail you're getting. My missus said why don't you have it sent round to the village hall? Plenty of rooms not used there.' He slurped his coffee.

'I'll think about it, Phil. Thank your wife for that suggestion.'

When Sally appeared in the doorway holding the box they stopped talking. She said, 'Sorry, Dad, I didn't know Phil was here.' She sat at the table with them.

Phil got up to go. 'My Missus said you should set up a group of people – like they do at the elections. She said she could arrange it for you.'

John went to the front door with him. 'I'll talk to the professor. He's receiving bags of mail too.'

In the kitchen, Sally saw the letter addressed to her from New York. Dwight had promised to write and he had. She slipped it into her dressing gown pocket.

John came back into the kitchen. He put bread into the toaster, saying, 'Must have something to eat this morning, Sally.' His voice was quite stern, he knew that, but he was worried about her, and not eating was not a good idea.

He sat at the table with her and noticed that the letter had disappeared. He said, 'Constable Evans will be here soon. He's taking us to the professor's. He's got something he wants to discuss with us.'

She nodded. John had given her a large glass of milk and two pieces of toast with butter and marmalade. Her favourite, but she was only pecking at it. And Ben's ashes lay on her lap.

He said, gently this time, 'How are you feeling this morning?'

She was very pale. 'I feel okay, Dad, I slept heavily last night.'

The sleeve of her dressing gown had slipped up and John could see the indentation marks on the underside of her arm from the box.

He desperately wanted to say something to her. The phone rang and he said he'd answer it and she was to finish her breakfast.

There was a lot of crackling and odd noises at the other end of the phone. Suddenly a voice said, 'Can I speak to Sally please?' It was Dwight, John recognised the voice. Sally was already at his side and grabbed the phone.

'Dwight? Is that you?' She sounded hysterical. They talked for a long time and John was relieved to see Ben's ashes had been left on the kitchen table.

33
The professor's place: early afternoon

THEY HAD GATHERED in the lounge, the professor, Mrs Gannon, Jamie, Sally and her dad. The box with Ben's ashes had been placed on a small table next to Sally. Much to the professor's relief no one had referred to it.

He went into his proposed plan for Mrs Gannon's mushrooms to be turned into a business concern in great detail. Jamie and Mrs Gannon had heard it all before and had to bear with him.

When he said, rather hesitantly, 'My plan is to involve the scope as well', Jamie said, 'You told us yesterday that it had been given to the police.'

'It has. I intend to design another one. Let me explain. We know what it is capable of, so I thought I'd use it to find out more about the mushroom.' He looked at them with a defiant expression.

Mrs Gannon shouted at him, 'Another contraption, Professor?'

He had great difficulty in holding his tongue when she used that crude word 'contraption'.

'That's right, Mrs G, another invention of mine. To study things we don't know about the mushroom.'

Sally intervened. 'Hasn't that been done before? It was on the telly.'

The professor coughed nervously, 'Up to a point, but there's always more to find out. We might make an amazing discovery. It will also mean a lot of note taking and record keeping.'

Mrs Gannon grunted and left the room.

'I can help with that,' Sally put in, 'if I could use your computer, Professor.'

Jamie said mournfully, 'So I'll be working in the cellar with Mrs Gannon?'

'That's right. Lifting and carrying the mushrooms and learning the business, Jamie – while I'll be doing the detective work.' The professor scrutinised his plan layout. Obviously, Jamie was not happy being down in the cellar with Mrs G. But when he knew the business they wouldn't have to be together on a regular basis. He'd think about it.

The sudden scream that enveloped the house had them all on their feet. The natural thing was to make for the door, but the professor stopped them in their tracks. It sounded like Mrs G. The screams drew nearer and she burst into the room so overcome that she couldn't speak.

Between them, John Gray and the professor got her to a seat. She was shaking.

'A brandy, pour her a brandy please,' the professor said. John had already done it, just a small one. He placed it in her shaking hand and she drank it in one go.

Jamie went to the windows to see if the bodyguards were still around. They were, and they were looking at the house and making calls on their mobiles.

'What is it, Mrs G?' the professor asked.

All she was able to do was point with a shaking arm.

The professor felt a chill run down his spine. Surely that scoundrel, Mario, wasn't back? No, he couldn't be, not with all the police protection. He said gently to her, 'Is it about our unwelcome visitor?'

'Unwelcome   visitor,'   Jamie   urged,   'what happened?'

The professor was loath to bring the subject up. 'Nothing happened – well, something did – Mrs G knocked him out with the scope.'

John Gray explained, 'It was when you were in New York. The professor had a visit from Mario.'

'If he was knocked out,' Jamie persisted, 'did you call the police?'

'Yes we did,' the professor said crossly, 'but he disappeared into thin air before they arrived. After that, you were kidnapped.'

The talk about Mario seemed to bring Mrs Gannon to her senses. She said, 'It's nothing to do with that – it's the mushrooms.'

Jamie ran from the room saying, 'I'll go down to the cellar to see what's wrong.' In the confusion Sally followed him, leaving Ben's ashes behind. John Gray took in a deep breath and thought 'It's just a matter of time'.

It didn't take them long to discover the mystery. Jamie and Sally were out of breath in their rush to get back.

'Well?' the professor asked.

Bewildered, Jamie said, 'They've grown!'

'That's what they're supposed to do,' the professor said.

'Big,' Jamie blurted out.

The professor clapped his hands. 'That's even better.'

Sally added, 'So big that some of them have ... ' She couldn't bring herself to say the word. She glanced at Ben's ashes and shouted it out, ' ... died.'

The professor hesitated, realising the emotional shock of the discovery. He thought quickly, and said, 'Impossible, they were perfectly healthy yesterday.'

Mrs Gannon was in floods of tears. She said, 'How can it be, Professor, after all the love and care I've given them?'

The professor rubbed his tummy and belched, something he normally never did in front of other people. He told Mrs G to calm herself; there must be an explanation for it. He fumbled around in his pockets and said, 'I think I must have left my indigestion powders in the cellar yesterday. Did you come across them, Mrs G?'

'Indigestion powders, what did they look like?' She got up and started to look round the room for them.

The professor, still rubbing his tummy, said, 'Just an ordinary small cardboard packet with indigestion powders written on the outside.' He belched again, much to his embarrassment.

Mrs Gannon gasped. She said, 'Oh, no, that's what happened!' The professor gave her a confused look. 'The powders,' she said. 'I couldnae find my spectacles yesterday and I needed to give the mushrooms some fertiliser. I must have thought that your powders – oh, no!'

She collapsed into her chair again and sobbed. The professor went to her and said, 'You thought my powders were your fertiliser?' She nodded.

He turned to Jamie and said, 'How many mushrooms have been affected, did you notice?'

Sally answered, 'Not all of them, about half perhaps.'

John Gray handed the professor a glass of water. He said, 'Well, all is not lost. Don't worry Mrs Gannon. We'll soon replace the lost ones with the help of your new assistants, not to mention the professor's scope.'

Mrs Gannon snorted. 'I don't know what the professor's contraption has got to do with it.'

With great dignity the professor rose from his chair and stood in front of her. He said, 'Well, let's say, my dear Mrs G, that my "contraption" has a way of seeing things that other people can't.'

He winked at Sally and Jamie and put his long thin arms round their shoulders. 'As from today,' he said, 'together, we are in business – the mushroom business!'

34
John Gray's cottage: late evening

IT HAD BEEN a long day. John sat in the kitchen sipping a beer. His eyes felt sore from too much daylight and he was glad to have the relief of the approaching night.

Many things had been discussed, including the huge amount of mail delivered daily to both houses. It had been agreed to take up Phil's offer to form a committee of local well-meaning people who wanted to help.

The setting up of the mushroom business was a bonus, he thought. Jamie and Sally in their enthusiasm were briefly relieved of the trauma that hung over their young heads. The professor was elected as Managing Director with research responsibility. At this point, Jamie and Sally would be learning the trade with Mrs Gannon's help; and, as an extra, Sally would have access to the professor's computer for the keeping of records, under his supervision. When the professor had suggested that John be employed as a night worker with a choice of a particular area, he had been pleasantly surprised. It was agreed that he would give his decision at their next meeting. The most important thing at the moment, John thought, was that Jamie and Sally had something to absorb their minds. The coming months would not be easy for any of them, especially the children. Ahead of them lay weeks of interviews with various police departments, and, when Mario was found, the trials.

Jamie fell asleep as soon as his head touched the pillow but Sally was wide awake. In the quietness of her small bedroom she slipped Dwight's letter out of her dressing gown pocket. Sitting on the edge of her bed she gazed at the envelope, afraid to open it. Her hands were shaking and she couldn't understand why.

Ben's ashes were on her pillow and she laid her head down to be close to him. She had got into the habit of whispering to him before going to sleep but tonight she found no solace. She told him about their day and the professor's idea to start a mushroom business. Always, how much she missed him, and it would end with a little prayer.

Angry with herself she sat bolt upright and tore the letter open. Dwight's writing was very neat, so much better than hers. Suddenly, her eyes filled with tears and the teardrops blurred his words. She shook the pieces of paper vigorously and blew on them, then laid them between her sheets, pressing down hard to absorb the wetness. Overcome with exhaustion, she ran to the bathroom and was sick.

In the kitchen John could hear his daughter vomiting. He wanted to tap on the bathroom door and ask if she was all right. But that would embarrass her and would only make things worse. She was at that awkward age and had been a victim of international espionage. That was more than enough for a twelve- year-old to cope with. He must give her space. He carried on washing the dishes before retiring himself.

When Sally crept back to her bedroom the shaking had stopped. Perhaps it was something she'd eaten.

Her tummy hadn't been right since being in New York.

She lifted the sheets and saw the smudged paper. At least it was only the top piece, she thought. And it wasn't all that bad. Dwight's writing was heavy and when she turned the smudged sheet over she could clearly see the indentation his pen had left on the back. She laid it down on her bedside table and lightly ran a pencil over the marks. The shape of the letters appeared and even though they were backwards she was able to decipher them.

Placing Ben's ashes on her windowsill she made herself comfortable and read:

'Hi Sal

I have to write in pen because Pop is using the computer all of the time. You said your writing wasn't good, do you remember? I said to you to use the computer, we both would – so, don't worry about me writing in pen will you?

I miss you guys so much, are you missing me? I was supposed to go to summer camp but that's been changed because of what happened to us. Pop said it wouldn't be safe for me to go and I have to be around when the police want to ask me questions. Have the police in London been asking you and Jamie questions?

I can't believe we were kidnapped and taken to Alaska. I've been having nightmares, so Pop lets me sleep in his room.

Do you like the photos I've sent you? The one of you on our balcony is my favourite, so I got it blown up and framed. I put it on my chest of drawers. I can lie in bed and look at you.

Pop said he spoke to Professor Venables on the phone and we're coming to see you soon, staying at the professor's house. Gee, I can't wait to see you again Sal. You are my girlfriend now aren't you? At first I didn't think Jamie liked me, but after what happened to us I got the feeling he did after all.

Ronnie is in a prison near us. She asked for me to visit her. I don't know what to think, she's my Mom and I suppose I should go. But I'm real nervous about it. Pop says there'll be a prison guard in the same room, so I don't have to worry. But it feels real odd as I never knew her. She left our place when I was only a year old. I feel like I've met someone from outer space who says they're my Mom. I won't know what to say to her. Perhaps she'll do all the talking, gee I hope so. I'm real nervous about the whole thing.

Pop gets all the London papers and we read them together. Our papers are full of the story as well. Loads of mail has been delivered to the NYPD for us. Pop and me go in and check it all out. We're lucky as Pop's got a team of police doing the sorting as there might be clues where Mario is.

There are some days when I get real bored. I can't go out and play baseball with my buddies without a police escort. Pop has the same problem as well. He can't even walk along to the diner for our food. He's collected every morning in an NYPD car and brought home.

Tomorrow I have to go and see my Mom. Pop said she'll be handcuffed and not to be upset about that.

He can't come with me because they're not allowed to talk to each other. But Pop said he doesn't mind. He said she's been gone for so long he'd almost forgotten what she looked like. He said she's done a bad thing being a spy, he said she's a traitor. That's a horrible word isn't it? In my nightmares I feel as if I've just watched one of those frightening space movies and people say things that aren't true and try to kill each other. It makes me scream and Pop holds me until I feel okay.

I was real upset when Pop said that Joe was a traitor too. He's in prison as well. I can't believe it because Joe was always good fun when I spent days at the NYPD. Do you remember him Sal? He showed you over the place and got you burgers and beans with chips in the canteen.

When I told Pop that we were sort of prisoners in a nice house in a cold country, he was very quiet. I told him Ronnie looked after us real good and gave us food we liked and that she had to take us to the store and buy warm clothes for us. I told him we thought it was Mario who was piloting the aircraft. And I told him about the fat woman who guarded us with a stick and we nicknamed her gorilla woman – that made him laugh.

I wish you weren't so far away Sal. Please write back to me quickly and show Jamie the photos.

If you can persuade the professor perhaps he'll let you use his computer so I can hear from you tomorrow – lots of love and hugs, Dwight.'

Sally carefully replaced the letter in its envelope. It was a lovely letter and she'd read it again in the morning. Now, she felt tired. Hearing from Dwight and reading his words was like being in the same room with him. She'd never been any good at writing compositions at school but there was a lot to talk about and she'd ask the professor to help her.

She slept so well that night that John had to tap on her bedroom door when she hadn't appeared by ten o'clock. There was no answer so he gently pushed the door open. She was peacefully asleep and lying under her cheek was the letter she'd received from New York.

35
The professor's place

IT WAS LUNCHTIME before they reached the professor's house. John had to phone Constable Evans to delay him coming at the usual time of ten. Jamie had been up for ages and said he was going to walk but the constable said that he mustn't do that.

Mrs Gannon was at the white gate looking down the hill. 'They should have been here ages ago,' she complained. 'I've got their jobs set out for them in the cellar. The mushrooms won't like it, they're used to proper timekeeping.'

'Mrs G,' the professor shouted from his hammock, 'your mushrooms will have to get used to a different routine. Like we all have had to do.'

That comment shut her up for a moment. Perhaps I am being a bit unreasonable, she thought. But it took quite a bit of generosity on her part to have her mushroom business taken over at such short notice.

At the sound of a car she was back at the gate. It was them. 'You're late,' she shouted.

The professor winced. The woman had no idea of what they'd been through. He waited patiently until John came over and helped him out of the hammock. He had his dark glasses on and was always polite and softly spoken – so different from Mrs G.

The first thing Jamie said to her was, 'What's for lunch, Mrs G?'

She stared at him and said, 'How dare you treat me like a servant? You are here to work this morning in the cellar – then you can eat.'

'But I'm hungry now. I won't work very well on an empty tum,' he retorted.

'That's enough,' Constable Evans said. He turned to the professor and suggested that they eat first. He also reminded him that they had to go through compiling of rotas, the day's delivery of mushrooms and collection of special compost.

'Thank you so much for reminding me, Constable.' The professor was pleased that this young man was taking an interest, despite the fact that he hadn't been asked. His job was to drive himself and the rest of them accompanied by police motor bikes.

Due to the constable's words the atmosphere had become sober and they automatically followed him into the dining room where, to the delight of all, Mrs Gannon had already laid out a splendid array of food from which to choose. To the constable's personal delight a large chocolate sponge sat in the centre of the table.

An agenda had been put together roughly by the professor during the night. It would be a working meal and he would preside.

It was quite a surprise when the professor announced his intention of converting the fields around his home into mushrooms units.

'Are the fields yours to build on?' John enquired.

'Oh yes,' the professor replied, 'The caravan site being one of them, alongside the huts which had housed prisoners of war of higher rank,' he added quickly. He glanced at Mrs G who, for once, was speechless.

Jamie said, 'What happens to the cellar, Professor?'

'That's where you'll learn the art of growing mushrooms under Mrs G's tutelage. There will be months of form filling and drawing up of plans to put forward to the Council. It won't happen overnight.' He looked again at Mrs G, who remained silent. He added for her benefit, 'The cellar will remain Mrs G's baby – her inheritance so to speak for having the initiative in the first place.'

The effect this had on her was startling. She rose from her chair like a phoenix. Her face was almost angelic and the professor could have sworn she floated round the room on the wings of a dove. But perhaps it was a mixture of sunlight and tiredness. He must remember to make an appointment with his optician.

Sally coughed to gain the professor's attention. She said, 'Can we look at the fields now? It's really exciting.' She knew about the caravan site and shuddered as the memories of Mario came back to her. But that must have changed now.

Constable Evans was keen to see the fields himself. The caravan site had been running successfully for a number of years. He knew the proprietor well and the professor's plans for the field's future would not bode well with him. He offered to drive them in his police car but first he would have to arrange for adequate plainclothes police officers to be present.

Mrs Gannon remained on cloud nine for the rest of the meal, disappearing to her kitchen and returning with yet another chocolate sponge. When they left to survey the fields not one crumb could be seen.

The professor's residence was large. It boasted at least six bedrooms and four bathrooms spread over three floors. Mrs G's quarters were at the back, next to the kitchen. She was so well settled in her bedsit that the professor was not sure he would be able to coax her out of it as her council flat in the village had already been let. But then, he mused, no one was going anywhere until 'Operation Lollipop' was solved.

The professor's own quarters were on the ground floor with a view of the gardens. All he needed was a bed in his large office with a bathroom attached. His laboratory was a no-go area and kept locked, although with the mushroom training for Sally and Jamie taking place soon he would have to allow them in.

When they eventually reached the campsite it was early evening. John was well protected from the sun and wore his dark glasses. He held a notebook and pencil to make notes, which impressed the professor. He also had the good manners to ask permission to make notes. He hadn't said any more about being one of the night workers at the mushroom farm, but the professor was confident that John would take up his offer.

Jamie hadn't been to the campsite that awful night when Sally and Ben had seen Mario and the other man, Frank, in the caravan talking about the professor.

When she saw it all again she went quite white. Nothing had changed. Her eyes scanned the field for the caravan next to the tall tree. The evening light was drawing in and John accompanied her while she studied the vans. Suddenly she stopped and turned her head away. 'It's that one Dad.'

John became her eyes. He said, 'By the tree?' She nodded.

The door was open and a man stepped out. He was tall and well dressed. He spoke to a couple who were passing, 'Nice evening, don't forget the Bingo tonight. Be there for six.' He locked the caravan door and walked in the direction of the site cafe.

'It's him,' she said. Her voice was hardly audible. John looked around for their bodyguards. He pointed in the direction the man had taken. They followed. He said quietly, 'Are you sure it's the man?'

She squeezed his arm and hid her face in his jacket. 'Yes, I only saw the back of him. Mario called him Frank. I told the police he was thin and tall and speaks posh. I forgot to tell them about the lisp. Did you hear it, Dad? I remember the lisp – always on his s's.'

John put his arm round his daughter. 'Yes, Sally, I heard the lisp too.'

The professor was taken up with showing the others around the huts. He had a large bunch of keys. He said 'The villagers use some of the units for meetings and evening classes. It suits me as they keep the buildings clean and my rent is negligible. Ideal, aren't they, for mushroom farming?'

When they came to the last unit, which was smaller in size, the professor had difficulty in unlocking the door. The key wasn't large like the others but more like a Yale key. He found one that worked. They were surprised with the inside. It had a fireplace, a carpet and two comfortable armchairs, a couple of small tables and a desk in a corner by a window. Behind a screen was a stove and sink. He said, 'I think we've invaded someone's privacy in here. It's obviously lived in.'

Jamie was poking around the desk, opening drawers. Mrs Gannon was pleased to sit down and Constable Evans was thinking they should join the others. Jamie went to get himself a drink of water. As he turned from the sink his sandal caught on something sharp. There was a mat on the floor but whatever was holding his sandal down was below it. He pulled hard and the whole thing came away, mat and part of the floor. He bent down to release his sandal strap from a latch in the rotting floorboards. It had left a gaping hole and Jamie could see that it was used to keep a case in.

He called to the professor and constable, 'Take a look at this.'

The professor said, 'We can't waste any more time in here, Jamie. Come along.'

Constable Evans casually walked round the screen and looked at the hole. 'That's been cut out for a purpose,' he said.

'It's got a case in it,' Jamie said, 'one of those posh cases.'

The constable looked closer, 'An attaché case.'

Mrs Gannon could hear what they were saying and took a look herself. 'If I'm not mistaken, Constable, that's the same case that Mario had.'

'Oh, why do you say that?' Constable Evans automatically took his black notebook from his pocket ready to take notes.

Mrs Gannon called to the professor. 'Come and look at this,' she said. 'What does it remind you of?'

The professor was getting exasperated with them. He said, 'We must go.' He squeezed into the small space behind the screen and took a quick look. 'It's a hiding place.'

'We know that,' Mrs G said to him. 'Take a closer look.'

He did, under great duress. He said, 'What am I supposed to be looking for?'

'That,' Mrs Gannon said, 'can't you see it?' She pointed to a long scratch mark below the handle.

'The leather is scratched ... it's scratched ... ' In the very limited space behind the screen he did a little jig and joyously shouted, 'My scope did that. I remember. After you hit Mario on the head, Mrs G, the scope dropped onto the case and scratched it at that very point.'

'Exactly,' Mrs G said.

Constable Evans took a pair of white gloves from his pocket and put them on. He lifted the case from its resting place and put it on the draining board. He groaned. 'Oh dear, it has a combination lock.'

'I'll force it for you,' Jamie suggested.

'Yes, do that, Jamie,' the professor said quickly.

Constable Evans intervened. He said, 'I can't allow that.' He raised his arm to stop Jamie.

'For Heaven's sake, why not?' The professor was furious.

'Because,' Constable Evans said, 'because, not only have we entered this room without the owner's consent, you are now suggesting we force open a case.' The constable placed the case back in the hole. He said, 'I suggest we leave.'

'This is ridiculous. You're quite wrong, Constable, I am the owner of these rooms and, therefore, have the right to enter.' The professor hesitated. He was angry and couldn't find the right words.

Constable Evans began ushering them out of the restricted space towards the door.

The professor was fiddling with the keys and Jamie was slightly ahead of him. In a flash, the professor grabbed him and slammed the door shut. He said, 'Quick, Jamie, get the case out of the hole and break it open.'

Outside, Constable Evans was banging on the door warning them that what they were doing was illegal.

The professor shouted back to him through the letterbox, 'I don't have time to be legal, Constable.'

Jamie found a box of tools under the sink and was forcing the lock. It didn't take long and when the lid flew open, he gasped. It was full of bank-notes. The professor nodded his head in delight. 'There is no doubt, Jamie,' he said, 'that this is the case Mario used to bribe me with.' Just to be sure, he opened a pocket inside the lid and took out a box. Inside was the hypodermic needle.

Jamie was awestruck by it all. He'd never seen so much money, except on the telly. The needle made him shudder.

The professor said calmly, 'Now, I'll let the constable and Mrs Gannon in.' He went to the door and unlocked it. Mrs Gannon was through the door first. She said, 'Well?'

The case had been placed on the desk in the corner of the room. When she saw it her excitement was so great that she threw her arms around the professor and hugged him. He had to fight her off.

Constable Evans took a camera from his jacket. He raced into the kitchen and began snapping away. 'This is evidence,' he shouted. This was followed by many snaps of the case open and shut. The alarm function on his walkie-talkie rang. It was John Gray. He said, 'Frank, Mario's accomplice, has just left the café. We're following him.'

All the plainclothes surveillance police on the caravan site had received the message too; there was a body of them. The two outside the room Professor Venables and his party were in had also been alerted.

The professor closed and locked the door as Constable Evans, Jamie and Mrs Gannon seated themselves and waited.

Outside, Frank, having been fed well in the café, made for his office. It had been a good day, he thought and tonight he looked forward to the Bingo session. He enjoyed his work with the holiday camps, especially the workshops he did with the kids. I should have been a teacher, he mused. He passed the friendly noises coming from the amusement arcade and the small fairground. Later, tonight, he would go to the ballroom dancing.

Gracie would be there and they would dance to the music of Glen Miller, his favourite.

He searched for the key in his immaculate suit, found it and unlocked the door. When he stepped in his eyes surveyed the scene in front of him. Without batting an eyelid he said, 'I wasn't expecting visitors.'

36
The professor's place

THEY MADE THEIR WAY back to the professor's house in a state of disbelief. The police had acted quickly. Frank had been arrested and taken to the local police station. A huge crowd of campers had gathered at the gates to wave him off, making it difficult for the police car to get through. The crowd shouted to him as he passed, 'Cheerio, Frank. It'll be all right. Don't worry.' He was very popular, and some of the campers were crying.

Frank smiled and waved to them as they crushed against the vehicle. He wanted to wind down the window and hold their hands, perhaps plant a kiss on a pretty face. But he was restrained.

Constable Evans dropped them off at the professor's house. 'I won't come in,' he said. 'They want my report at the station.'

The professor nodded wearily. What a day it had been – and this was only the beginning. There's going to be weeks of interviews and reports, he mused. He made a point of going to the constable's car window to enquire if they were still being given police protection now that Frank had been arrested. The constable assured him they were.

'I'll let the others know,' the professor said. 'It will be the first thing they ask when I get inside the house.'

'I'll see you tomorrow, Professor.' The constable drove off at some speed, causing a swirl of dust to rise in his wake.

No sooner was the professor's foot through the front door when the phone began to ring. That'll be Captain Murphy, he thought. Mrs Gannon got to the phone before he did. He was right, it was Murphy. 'I'll take the call in my study, Mrs G, if you would be good enough to pass me the instrument.' Pouting, she did so. He also added, 'A nice cup of tea would be most welcome for all of us, thank you, Mrs G.'

In the quiet and coolness of his study the professor made himself comfortable for what was bound to be a long spiel from the Captain.

Murphy was making the call from his apartment. He was shouting down the line, 'Professor, are you there?'

'Yes, I'm here, Captain Murphy. I imagine you've heard the latest news from London?' As he spoke, the professor rested his tired legs on a pouffe.

'I've just picked it up on my car radio, Professor. I'll be flying over tomorrow with Dwight. Is that okay with you?'

The professor hadn't expected this reaction from Murphy. He had to think quickly. He spluttered, 'No problem, Captain, I'll get Mrs G to make up a room for you both.'

'Look forward to seeing you Professor,' Murphy said. 'Arresting Mario's accomplice is a starter. Let's hope he talks.' The phone went dead.

The professor opened the French doors and stepped into the garden. They were waiting for him on the veranda. A table had been laid for a casual evening meal of salad and sandwiches. And there, in the centre, was a large chocolate sponge cake. It's a pity that Constable Evans isn't with us tonight, he thought.

Someone had erected a gazebo over the table. The professor had forgotten he had one. He was pleased as it gave extra protection for John. He'd taken a liking to Sally's dad and had already decided that he'd be an asset in the expansion of the mushroom business, especially in his laboratory.

Mrs G handed him a plate of cucumber sandwiches – his favourite, how kind of her. His eyes roamed round the table. Incredible, he mused, I have inherited a family. Sally was on his right next to Jamie. She must have left Ben's ashes in the lounge. Next to Jamie was John Gray, in a shaded area. He had further protection from the light by a splendid tree in full blossom, its branches gently tapping the gazebo in the breeze. Next to John sat Mrs G, hovering over them like an old mother hen. The chair next to Mrs G's was empty. Perhaps Constable Evans would turn up later. No, he was wrong. When the warm breeze riffled the table-cloth, he saw Ben's ornamental box on the seat. It was a round table, so they were all equal, the professor reflected – even Ben.

When the last of the chocolate sponge had been eaten and the teapot emptied the professor tapped on his plate. He said, 'As a result of today's events at the holiday camp, Captain Murphy will be flying over to London tomorrow. He will be my guest here. We will be kept very busy and you must make sure you are here to answer questions. Kidnapping in the USA is a federal offence and the FBI will be involved, along with the appropriate department of Scotland Yard.'

Sally asked, 'What about Dwight? Will he be coming too?'

'Yes, he will be coming. Constable Evans and Captain Murphy will be expecting written reports, especially about what happened prior to the kidnap in Central Park and ... ' The professor paused for a moment before adding, ' ... and what happened leading up to Ben's death.'

In her anguish to escape, Sally's chair was thrown down as she grabbed Ben's ashes and ran from the veranda. The professor's heart sank. He said quietly, 'We'll talk later – when she comes back.'

Sally crept upstairs. There was a small room at the back of the house. She slipped through its door and locked herself in.

It was cosy and safe. Many days she'd come here without the others knowing, especially if Jamie and Ben were having a quarrel. She sat on the floral duvet. The matching curtains were closed so she pulled them just a little bit open.

She took the screwed-up letter she'd written to Dwight out of her pocket. He'll be here tomorrow. I can give it to him, she thought. She started to read it in a whisper. Suddenly she stopped. Lifting Ben's ashes off the floor she placed them on the windowsill so she would be facing him. That's better. A little gleam of sunlight shone on its beautifully carved lid. She started again.

'Dear Dwight, I was so pleased to get your letter and the photos. You took lots. They're like a story only in pictures of all those people in Central Park and the hangar. I didn't see you taking them. The inside of the plane is a super photo. Even the gorilla woman looks great. Good thing she was asleep.

Where did you hide your camera? The one of Ronnie doing cheese on toast is my favourite. And how did you get into her locked room? Don't know why you took photos of all that foreign writing and numbers.

Dad let me use his computer to write this. He helped with my spelling.

The photo of Ben lying in the hospital bed is beautiful. I look at it a lot because he looks so peaceful. I take his ashes everywhere with me. I don't want him to be lonely. Then I look at your photo again and think perhaps that's how he'd want it – peaceful.'

She placed the unfinished letter on the floor to press out the creases with her hand.

Afterwards

Much to the professor's astonishment, Frank was released from prison because of lack of evidence against him. The contents of the hypodermic needle revealed that it contained only a mild sleeping draught. Frank insisted that he was looking after the attaché case for a friend. When the police went to retrieve it the money had disappeared. It couldn't have been Frank as he was in prison, so it was probably Mario.

Ronnie remained imprisoned after the gang's written reports were read out at the Hearing in New York. Dwight went through a bad time coping with it – she was his mom. Joe remained imprisoned too.

Mario was never found. Ronnie had written a letter to Dwight saying that he'd been planning to retire after the kidnapping episode. He was a very rich man and had had extensive cosmetic surgery on his face. He'd also changed the colour of his hair and would be unrecognisable.

As soon as the campsite had been cleared by the police, Professor Venables converted the huts into perfectly controlled housing for mushroom cultivation. Sally and Jamie were over the moon with their new-found jobs and Mrs Gannon wondered how on earth she'd managed before.

John Gray took up the professor's offer of assisting in the laboratory; and when Dwight visited from New York in school holidays, he helped too. His friendship with Sally grew, as did the mushroom business.

To overcome his disappointment about Sally, Jamie worked longer hours; and when he reached sixteen, the professor employed him full time.

By the time Sally was sixteen her knowledge of compost preparation, temperature and humidity control to avoid disease in the crops, was praiseworthy. So the professor employed her full time as a trainee supervisor. Without fail, every week she would polish Ben's box and talk to him about the mushrooms.

When he was eighteen, Dwight won a scholarship to study forensic science in London. Captain Murphy was really proud of his son. They flew over to visit the professor. During their stay, Dwight asked Sally to marry him when he'd finished his studies. She was very happy, and the professor and Mrs G threw an engagement party for them. Jamie pretended everything was great, but inside his heart was broken.

When Sally was twenty-five, she and Dwight married in the village church. Jamie was best man and John Gray, wearing his dark glasses, proudly walked his daughter down the aisle. The little church was packed, and crowds, including newspaper reporters, were waiting outside. People had remembered.

A year later, Sally gave birth to a baby boy. Dwight knew what was in her mind. As he proudly cradled his baby son, he said, 'We'll call him Benjamin, and Woodrow after my Pop.'

'And,' Sally whispered, 'John, after my dad. Benjamin, Woodrow, John – all American Presidents.'

'Just what I was thinking,' Dwight whispered back. He lay down on the bed beside her, the warm bundle between them. He kissed her cheek and said, 'I love you Sally Murphy, and little Benjamin loves you even more, if that's possible.'

Sally asked the professor if the oak tree between his garden and the mushroom farm could be dedicated to Ben. He was delighted, and said, 'I'll ask the vicar to preside over a little service.'

She added quickly, 'That's very kind of you, Professor, but I'd prefer something more personal. You see, Ben spent many happy hours climbing it and being able to see for miles. Just you and Mrs G, Dad of course, Jamie, Dwight and his dad – and I thought Constable Evans.'

The professor nodded in understanding. He'd climbed that old oak tree when he was a boy.

The dedication was short and simple. Jamie had been down earlier to prepare a small resting-place. The day was sunny and warm and wild flowers danced in the breeze, while the group around the oak tree felt a sense of comfort as Ben's ashes were laid to rest.

ʰtning Source UK Ltd.
ㄱ Keynes UK
ᴐ51138111112

ᶠUK00005B/18/P